Hypnotized By A Savage 3
Nayh Alontrice

Previously...

We pulled up in front of Sullivan's Steakhouse and found a park closer to the door. He came on my side and opened the door for me. My black Giuseppe heels were all you could hear as we made our way inside of the restaurant.

Stopping at the host podium, "Hello, I have a reservation for Bonnie Jones."

"Yes ma'am, it'll be right this way. Follow me."

The host grabbed four menus, and my eyebrow rose because it should only be three menus needed. When we got to our table, I kept my poker face on, but I was irritated because I didn't get the memo that we were having additional guests. When Micah said he was coming with me, no ifs, ands, or buts about it, I immediately informed Miguel of that by text.

"Hello Bonnie, you're looking beautiful as always." Miguel smiled, reaching for my hand to kiss it.

"She's cool, bruh. Who's this?" Micah asked. If looks could kill, Miguel wouldn't even be breathing right now.

"Oh, I'm Rich. I'm surprised Bonnie never talked about me," Rich replied.

"I mean, what would I have to speak about you? We do business. That's it. I'm assuming that's why you're at this meeting," I fired back. I don't know what the fuck they had planned, but I had enough shit on my plate to have to deal with this.

"Bonnie, it's not like that honestly. Why don't you have a seat? We don't want to cause a scene in here." Miguel spoke in a serious manner. Micah pulled out my chair and then sat down next to me.

"What's this about, Miguel? Because honestly, I have so much shit going on and people trying to come against me, I don't know if I can handle y'all being on bullshit too."

"We're here to show you our loyalty. We wanted to personally let you know that no matter what, we're on your side. We both got a visit from Laina Rodriguez, offering us your spot, but we turned her down. Our belief in your organization is what made that decision for us. You have Rich in Atlanta, me in New York, Chico in Chicago, and soon enough, you'll have someone in Miami as well," Miguel mentioned.

"Who's in Miami?"

"Her name is Mercedes Rosales. Now, I know you tend to think no one can be on your level, but trust me, she's a unique one."

"I'm all for women empowerment — the more women, the better. It's a little too much testosterone around me already." I was grateful that I had people who continued to stay down with me.

"Okay, cool, y'all don't know how much I appreciate you having my back. I don't know what Laina's problem is, but her best bet is to keep my name out her mouth."

I was furious. This bitch had the audacity to try to take shit away from me. Like, bitch, you're a woman first. Why would you try to stop the next woman's shine? I was so confused and upset.

"Didn't you say your daddy learned from Diego? Why don't he go and visit Diego to see what's up with his wife?" Micah asked me.

"Good idea, bae. That sounds like a plan. I'mma call him as soon as we leave here. The crazy thing is y'all bringing this news to me, and she also went to Casino telling him the same thing. According to Nookie, he's really considering it."

"Aww well, ain't no questions as to what needs to happen next, I'll have my shooters come and take care of him," Rich responded.

"Wait, wait, first off, we don't need no shooters. I can handle that shit, and secondly, Casino is like my brother. He knows he'd be going against the grain coming at Bonnie," Micah expressed.

"Well, I guess, I'll give you a chance to talk to him, but trust, if he goes on the side of the opposition…"

"Then, his ass is outta here," Micah finished my sentence.

"With that being said, raise ya glasses. We about to take this shit over and all the appreciation goes to Bonnie for inviting us into this power circle."

We all held our glasses up as Rich spoke. I didn't bring up me quitting because my adrenaline was up now, and I was ready to take mafuckas out, then I'd quit…

Chapter 1: Bonnie

"Your Honor, this is blasphemy! The prosecutors are simply pinning whatever they can on my client because she did not agree to be a criminal informant in their case against Diego Rodriguez! I mean, she never even had a record for crying out loud."

I sat watching patiently as my lawyer and the prosecutor were going toe-to-toe.

"Your Honor, we are asking that bail be denied. We have substantial information from one of our fellow police officers that went undercover. His testimony alone could put her away for life. Her not having a record means nothing. That just means she knows how to get around the system."

The prosecutor looked over at me, I gave her one of the deadliest looks ever, and then I smirked.

"Well, I hear what you're saying Counselor Guthrie, BUT this isn't the trial yet, and as far as I can see, you all don't have any substantial evidence present NOW. Do you?" Judge Matthews questioned.

"No, Your Honor, we don't. They are still gathering all the information from him being undercover. However, we are holding her on charges for homicide and the distribution of narcotics. She is not someone who needs to be out in the public eye until it's proven that she's innocent."

The prosecutor was turning red in the face, and I enjoyed every minute of it. I looked back behind and smiled big when I saw

Micah, Nookie, and Casino staring back at me. They were supporting me by calling and making sure money was on my phone, even though I was only here for a couple of weeks. My lawyer assured me that he'd get me out on bail, and I was excited because I had a life to get back to.

"Enough. There will be no more argumentative stances from you, Counselor Guthrie. Now, Mr. Hayes, the defendant's bail will be set at $100,000. This case is adjourned." He banged his gavel and departed from the stand.

"Thank you so much." I shook hands with Don and smiled.

"No problem, the judge was on our side today, I'll tell you more once we're done here. Enjoy it and try to be on your best behavior," he smirked.

The officers came and started to take me away.

"Wait, ain't I'm free now?" I asked my lawyer.

"Well, you all have to post the bail first, Bonnie. Just a few more hours and you'll be good to go."

"Get on it, baby!" I shouted as they walked me back into the holding cell.

I was ecstatic because I was grateful that I didn't have to waste any more time here because I could've been planning my damn wedding. The officers sat me down on the bench right across from this light-skinned bitch who had been mugging me since we got off the paddy wagon. I was trying my best to ignore the bitch, but I see I was gon' have to check her ass because I felt her eyes burning a hole in my face.

"Bitch, is there something you wanna say to me?" I asked her.

"Oh, so now you don't know who I am? Bitch, you ain't that high up to where you don't recognize us little people anymore." The girl had so much hatred in her voice.

"Bitch, I've barely even looked at you. How would I know who you are? And I have never been the type to look down on mafuckas because I'm that bitch, I don't have to do the extra shit."

"Fuck you, Bonnie. My life has been ruined ever since I've met you in high school. I always played second fiddle when it came to you, and now suddenly you and the nigga I was fucking are engaged!"

I rolled my eyes once I figured out who it was. I thought this bitch had disappeared, and now I end up in a holding cell with the bitch. She looked completely different from how she looked ten months ago. As far as I'm concerned, after I told her to flee, she became nonexistent to me.

"Chandlyn, girl, are you really sitting here being bitter about shit? And ain't you supposed to be far the fuck away? Last time I checked, Micah was a single man when I met him. Just because you were getting dick from him, don't make y'all committed to each other. Therefore, it was fair game. And as far as high school, all the shit you went through was because of YOU. Don't blame me for the shit."

I was irritated to the max, this bitch had the nerve to come for me, and all I did was try to put her in the game with me. She couldn't do the shit, and I didn't want to leave her out to dry, so I made her one of my girls at the warehouse, and even that went downhill.

Sniffing, Chandlyn voiced, "Yeah, okay, Bonnie. You always right, huh? Even if I didn't work for you, you coulda continued to be friends with me. Nookie didn't have to, so don't forget how much I fucking know. You're in here for a reason, and I can make sure you never get out."

Chandlyn was crying, but from the look on her face, I knew this bitch would rat me out. I'd play nice for now, but the moment I'm out, she got to go, and I won't be the one getting my hands dirty to do it.

Chapter 2: Micah

I was happy as hell the judge approved Bonnie to get out on bail. These last couple of weeks has been tough without her, real talk. I can't imagine how she feels because she had so many plans, but everything just seemed to be falling apart. This could be what I've tried to tell Bonnie all along. This being in the game shit must end. We are more than comfortable money-wise, and I know it's gonna be hard, but she needs to do what's best for our soon-to-be family and us. I never thought I'd be the type of nigga to get ready to settle down and get out of the game. It was fast money and honestly fun as hell, whether it was getting paid to commit murder or making money selling drugs. However, I met somebody who made me want to change all that shit. I was ready to have kids and build as a family. Eventually, I'd build something that would display my mother's memory, and I want to pass that on to my children.

Walking out of the bail bondsman's office, I saw somebody standing up against my truck. I marched over there pissed off because I had time for nobody's bullshit today.

"Aye, get the fuck up off my shit."

"Tsk, tsk, you may wanna lose your attitude, homeboy." The nigga moved his suit jacket to the left and revealed his badge and gun.

"Who are you, and what the fuck you want?"

"I just wanted to ask you a couple of questions. I see you made sure your fiancée won't be sitting for too much longer."

"That pertains to you, why?" I asked.

"Well, I have a way of helping her if you wanted to consider it?"

"I thought you had a couple of questions? Right now, it looks like you offering services and shit." I was very irritated.

"I know the guy who went undercover against her. I could help you get rid of him for a fee." He pulled out a pack of Newports and offered one to me. I declined, so he took one out and lit it up.

"Damn, there ain't a good cop left in Indianapolis, huh? Here you are, offering to end one of your own. Do y'all even know what loyalty is?" I chuckled.

Blowing out smoke in my direction, he retorted, "My loyalty is to my family and providing a life for them that's stable."

"No, thank you, we don't need that type of assistance."

I tried to get in through the driver's side, but he blocked me. My jaw clenched because this mafucka didn't know who I was, I'd end his life right here and now. I wouldn't even give a damn about anybody seeing me.

He pulled out a card and extended it to me.

"If you change your mind, here's my name and number. FYI, Bonnie can get out on bail, but that won't stop them from making sure she never sees daylight again once the trial begins."

I took the card, and he walked away. I just shook my head because mafuckas was bold nowadays, but I tucked that card in my pocket because I needed a backup plan, and he'd be just that. If we can get somebody to get rid of Reaper and not get our hands dirty, that'd be perfect.

***

I figured I'd go meet up with Casino and Nookie at they crib while waiting for them to release Bonnie. I saw another car outside and hoped it wasn't anybody that was secretively plotting since that's all we've been coming across. I parked and rang the doorbell once I reached the door.

"Hey, it's Micah y'all," Nookie said as she moved to the side to let me in.

"Wassup, sis? I see my nephew, poking out a little. I ain't notice it at court because you were sitting down." I hugged Nookie.

Laughing, Nookie voiced, "No, your niece is poking out. We will find out in a couple of weeks. Hopefully we get a lot of good news that day because you know since the attack, they've had me come in every week to make sure the placenta is still intact."

"It's gonna be all good, sis. I know it will."

I scanned the living room, and Casino and Star were sitting on the couch while CJ was snuggled against her. I'm just looking confused because I'm wondering why Nookie was cool with how close they were. What surprised me, even more, was how Nookie went on the other end, and Casino wrapped his arm around her.

I cleared my throat. "Yo, Casino, can I holler at you for a minute?"

"I got you, bro." He got up, and Star moved closer to Nookie. I followed him to the back and once we were in his office, I closed the door.

"Damn nigga, you got it like that?" I asked him.

"Mannnn, this shit wild, ain't it? I swear I did not see the shit coming. Nevertheless, I love Nookie, and Nookie loves men and women. At first, after that Toya shit, I was shitty about it, but it being my baby mama makes shit a little different you feel me?" He was smiling hard as hell as he explained it.

"Damn, so this was sis' idea?"

"Yes, nigga, I'm following her lead, and I can't lie and say the shit ain't been lovely. Even with being able to see my son every day, it's amazing."

"I hear that, bro. Y'all know I'm rocking with y'all 100%. I can't wait to see how Bonnie reacts to this shit." I laughed.

"Aww shit, ain't no telling bro. I'mma let Nookie deliver the message about that. Wassup though? They release her yet?"

"Hell nah, I'm waiting on that call now. After we all left the city's county building, I went straight to the bail bondsman to bail her out. We're in the waiting game now."

"Shit, that's all that matters then. Now that they got the money, they can't do shit but release her."

"When I walked out from paying the bond, this nigga was leaning on my truck and shit. You know I don't play that shit. I was about ready to put one in his dome."

"Who the fuck was it?"

"Some FED ass nigga showed me his badge and shit talking about for a fee he'd get rid of Reaper."

"On everything? Damn, what the hell?"

Nodding my head yes, I added, "Real shit, bro. The mafuckas with IMPD ain't shit. You show them you got a little of money and they gon' flip on each other."

"That may not be a bad idea, though. Let somebody else get rid of that rat ass nigga. Bonnie would be in the clear fasho."

"Right, that's the prosecutor's only evidence. I'm really thinking about the shit, my nigga. I just don't want shit to go wrong even more once that nigga turns up missing."

"Lemme know what you do, my nigga. I do think he needs to be eliminated because it seems like he was with Bonnie through every move she made when y'all was apart."

Casino made a good point because if we would've stayed together, that nigga wouldn't have been in the picture. Bonnie was the one that was afraid of commitment, but I understood her point.

My phone started ringing. I got anxious because that meant it was time for my baby to be picked up.

"Hello?"

"Hi, is this Micah?

"Yeah, who's this?"

"Yes, we need your assistance with identifying a body. There was no identification on the victim, but there was a phone in the wrecked car. It was only a few contacts in there, and you were one of them."

"What happened to the other contacts that were in there?"

"One line was disconnected, and the other line went to voicemail. We left them a message."

"Okay, what's the location?"

"4011 S. Monroe Medical Park Boulevard. Bloomington, Indiana."

"BLOOMINGTON? Who the hell did I know in Bloomington?"

"I understand it may take up some time, but whenever you can in the next 48 hours, we'd appreciate the assistance."

"Okay, I'll see what I can do."

I hung up the phone and had a bewildered look on my face.

"Who was that, bro?" Casino asked.

"Shit, I gotta go identify a body, but who the fuck is it?"

Chapter 3: OG

I was upset with myself because I felt like I had let Bonnie down once again. She was taking after the life that I had, and that's what I didn't want to happen. At least not the way the shit was going. It was all my fault. The moment she asked me to teach her the methods to the game, I should've decided against it. However, she had just lost her mother, and I lost my wife. I knew that us bonding while I taught her the ropes would help with us grieving. I regretted it all now.

I was in Miami, preparing to end Jose's life. This was the bastard who ratted Diego out and ultimately planned to bring the entire organization down with what he knew. With him gone, there would be no chance of additional evidence against my daughter. I honestly didn't know if he had even talked to the FEDS at all, but I couldn't take that chance. Diego had already let me know wassup with Jose, and it was always better to shoot first and ask questions later. There was no reason Diego would pinpoint him out if he didn't have proof. I had been watching this nigga for about three weeks now, and he really thinks he can't be touched.

He stayed clubbing at Club LIV every night and leaving with a different broad each night. This nigga must not know that bitches rob mafuckas too nowadays. Word around the city is that he has everybody scared of him. I saw right through that shit, though. Jose didn't know that anyone knew that he was a snitch. Diego confided in me that he knew who it was, and I planned to punish this nigga for flipping on him. Diego's always been down for anybody that was straight up with him. He doesn't deserve to rot in jail.

Earlier today, I had this fine, Latina chick in my bed, only because a nigga got needs. I gotta do what I gotta do. Nonetheless, shawty thought we were about to lay up and shit, nah, I wasn't with that. So, what I decided to do was get her on board with my plan. I paid for her to get dolled up so that she could go to the club tonight because I knew that nigga was gon' be there. After she lured him to the hotel, I'd be there and come up from behind them when they hop out the car. If everything goes right, this nigga would be spending his last night on earth, so he'd better enjoy it.

***

"You really think the plan will fall through?" she asked.

"It should. If you do your part right, everything should be good to go."

"Yeah, but I haven't heard good things about him on the streets. What if something happens to me?"

"Mercedes, I got you. Nothing is going to happen to you. That's one thing for sure. It'll look like a robbery, if anything. He won't know you were part of it."

"Okay, I just had to make sure. I'll make sure I put some extra spice on it. He'll have no choice but to invite me back." She smiled.

I walked to the door and rolled my eyes as she followed close behind. This girl really thought we were going to pursue something after all this. I'mma throw her a couple thousand and be on my way back to Nap.

***

I locked eyes with Mercedes on the dance floor. I was up on the second floor leaning off the rail near the VIP area. I nodded my head towards Jose and his crew. They were to the left of me enjoying themselves. She started heading towards the stairs that led up to us. Once she made it, she didn't even go to VIP. She just started dancing and letting her hands roam all over her body. Mercedes was fine as hell. She reminded me of Dascha Polanco. She just wasn't as thick as her.

I could see Jose staring at her from the corner of my eyes. I smirked and made my exit to prepare myself. I planned to already be at the hotel once they arrived, so I had to leave the club well before they did. Once I was outside, I hopped in the rental I got when I came here and sped off. I told her to choose the Palms Hotel & Spa because it was one of the closest to the club.

Waiting for her to give me the word, I decided to clean my weapons. I popped the trunk and hopped out of the car. I retrieved the briefcase and got back inside. My smile grew big as I opened it up. I had all types of weapons here just in case I didn't know which way to kill a mafucka. I had a machete, .9mm, Taser, and switchblade. Shit, I even had a grenade in that mafucka. My shit was top of the line because I had connections with a lot of people, especially people in the military and shit.

My phone buzzed, and I was hoping it was Mercedes. It wasn't her. It was Casino.

"Wassup, youngblood?"

"Shit, not much, was just letting you know Bonnie was released on bail. Micah paid that shit about an hour ago, but they still haven't released her."

"That's good that they let her out on bail. Make sure y'all tell her I'm sorry I couldn't be there, but I promise I'm on a mission that's gonna help."

"I got you, OG. Bonnie gon' be good. You ain't even gotta worry. She knows you're doing what's best. Aye, it is something I wanted to talk to you about. Micah got a call from the morgue at the Monroe Hospital in Bloomington. They say he needs to identify a body."

"Shit, how would I know?"

"I mean you remember a few months ago what happened with his uncle, I thought maybe you'd know some other shit."

"Nah, not this time, youngblood. I personally saw Sleepy in the casket myself, so I know that nigga is six feet under."

"Damn, you done went to see the nigga you killed? You're one cold mafucka.

"Don't you forget it."

My phone vibrated, I looked and saw it was Mercedes. The text read, "*It's a go.*"

"Youngblood, I'll hit you up later. Tell Bonnie to call me as soon as she can.

"Aight one."

It was showtime. I grabbed the .9mm, screwed the silencer on, and I tucked it into my waistband. All those other weapons would come in handy once I got Jose secluded. She shot me another text that said, "*All-black suburban.*" Another idea came to my head once she told me that. I sent her another text back that read, "*Hop in the rental, I'mma take the Suburban.*"

Like clockwork, they pulled up. I got out smoothly and started walking up behind the truck. The driver opened his door and was about to open the back door to let Jose out, but I popped him right in between his eyes. He was at the wrong place at the wrong time, collateral damage.

"What the fuck? What's taking you so long to open the door?" Jose popped his door open, and I pointed the gun right at his face, "Oh shit, man, who you?"

"Don't worry about all that stand the fuck up!" I ordered.

He got out the truck, and I started patting him down.

"Pussy ass nigga, you don't even have a gun on you? You think you that hard, huh?" I popped him in the face with the back of my .9mm, and he started crying like a bitch, "Get back in the truck."

I locked eyes with Mercedes and gave her a wink. She opened the door and ran out, probably to make it look like she was getting away.

"Damn bitch, you gon' leave me?" Jose yelled.

"Shut the fuck up, nigga."

I grabbed the zip ties out my pocket and placed two on his hands and his ankles. I had to double them because if this nigga got away, I was gon' be pissed. Matter a fact that wasn't enough. I needed this nigga to be knocked out or paralyzed for a little. I tased his ass and hopped in the driver seat. I was ready to make sure this nigga never flipped on anyone ever again. He was in for a rude awakening because I was about to take all my aggression out while torturing his ass.

Chapter 4: Star

It felt so good being around Chase a lot more. I had to admit that I didn't expect Nookie to be so open with me coming around, but when I found out why she was cool with it, it all made sense. It was just crazy because the very thing that Chase claimed broke us up is what brought us back together, another woman. I was afraid all of this would confuse CJ, but he seemed to be doing okay. He didn't really ask any questions. He was probably just happy waking up to both of his parents every day. I still had my apartment just in case this shit went downhill. My phone rang while we were watching *Love & Hip-Hop Hollywood*, so I sent them to voicemail. If it were important, they'd leave a message.

A good thirty minutes went by, and my phone vibrated. It was a voicemail, so I opened it up and my phone was transcribing the message. Once it was complete, all it took for me to read was "identify a body" for me to jump up and go into the bathroom to call the place back. I dialed the number back so fast. I was afraid of what the person on the other line had to say, but I needed to know what this was about.

"Monroe Hospital, how can I direct your call?"

"Umm, yes, someone left me a voicemail stating they needed me to identify a body."

"One moment, please."

I scratched my head because I was just puzzled as to who this could be. It was time for Nookie to get me in her chair too because I heard she was a cold stylist. This was the best shit ever having a three-way relationship with a hairdresser.

"This is Dr. Dandridge; how can I assist you today?"

"Someone mentioned identifying a body on my voicemail."

"Oh yes, is this Star?"

"Yes."

"We found a cell phone in a wrecked vehicle where we found the body, and you were one of the contacts in there out of three. We found someone to identify it, though."

"May I ask whom?"

"A guy named Micah. I just got off the phone with him not too long ago. Thank you for your time, though, and sorry for the inconvenience."

I hung up the phone and just stared at the wall. Who in the hell could it be that Micah and I know? I haven't even talked to Micah on a personal level in years. I heard Casino and Micah walking out of his office and saw the perfect chance to pick Micah's brain to see if he knew. I walked out of the bathroom and followed them into the living room.

"Micah, did you get a call about identifying a body?" I asked him.

"Damn, you got bionic ears or something? How'd you know that?" he questioned.

"Because I was one of the people they called too. We were watching the show, and I didn't recognize the number, so I sent them to voicemail. I just called them back, though, and that's when she told me she talked to you already."

We all were in the living room, staring at one another.

"Wow, this shit's weird. I guess we ain't got no choice but to see what the fuck is going on." Casino scratched his head.

"And when do y'all plan on doing that? Bonnie is going to get released soon, and we have to get her as soon as she calls." Nookie stated.

"That's right. Well, Micah, do you just want me to go and find out? I know you've been waiting for this moment for two weeks. I gotta a feeling she will be outraged if you're not the one to pick her up," I offered.

"Shit, that's gon' have to be the plan because I ain't tryna mess up none of our wedding vibes. I'd be starting off wrong already. Just call me when you find out who the hell it is."

"Road trippppp!" Nookie said.

"Bloomington's only like an hour away." Casino said.

"I know, but it'll be fun, you know I like riding." Nookie blushed.

"On that note, I'll holla at y'all later on." Micah laughed as he walked out the door.

I guess we were taking a little road trip because I needed to find out who was dead as soon as possible.

***

We pulled up to Monroe Hospital in about 45 minutes, thanks to Chase's psychotic driving.

"If y'all don't mind, I would like to go see who it is myself first."

"Go ahead, we'll be right out here if you need us, love." Nookie was so sweet. I was beginning to develop strong feelings for her. I always wondered if you could be in love with two people. I guess I'll find out soon enough.

I got out of the backseat and headed inside the hospital.

Stopping at the receptionist's desk, I voiced, "Hello, I'm here to identify a body."

"Okay, the first thing you'll do is go to the elevator over to your left and go to the basement. It should be straight ahead once you get off," the receptionist said.

"Thank you," I said as I followed the directions that she gave me.

When I walked into the morgue, I immediately got an eerie feeling. I was a person who didn't even like scary movies. This was spooky to me, but curiosity got the best of me. I walked in and didn't see anyone.

"Hello?" I yelled out.

A white lady walked out from the back. "Hi, yes, what can I do for you?"

"I'm here to identify a body. Micah had another obligation he had to tend to," I replied.

"Okay, that's perfectly fine. You must be Star. Follow me," she said.

We walked through the double doors that led to the back. Once we reached the correct spot, my body got chills. It was just like in the movies and shit. I saw the multiple silver doors that held dead bodies. She stopped in front of the one that was dead in the middle.

"Now, I want you to prepare yourself. Half of the face is severely burned, but you should still be able to make out who the person is from the other side."

"Got it."

She grabbed the handle, and I swore that everything felt like it was going in slow motion. When she pulled the drawer out, I saw that the person had no hair or not much of it was left. I stared down at the body and shook my head. Even though we didn't really stop talking based on good terms, I never wanted to see her dead. I did share some of my most intimate stories and even messed around with her a couple of times. It was crazy that you could be here one day and gone the next in the blink of an eye.

"Do you recognize her, ma'am?" Dr. Dandridge asked.

"Yes, unfortunately, I do. That's my friend Toya, Toya Walker."

I couldn't believe it but saying her name made it even more real. A tear dropped from my eye because even though she meant so much to me at some point, I was happy that she'd be out of the picture. Yes, her death was unexpected, but what she did to Nookie was uncalled for and according to Nookie, Toya has made her life a living hell. It was cool, though, because now she'd get to see that Toya wouldn't be a problem anymore.

Chapter 5: Nookie

"So, what you think about our arrangement so far?" I asked Chase as we were outside of the hospital waiting for Star to come back out. I looked in the backseat and saw CJ sound asleep.

"You want me to be honest or tell you what you wanna hear?" he responded.

"Be honest, babe."

"I'm like the happiest nigga ever shit. I know you probably expected me to not allow this shit because of the Toya situation, but this my baby mama. She will always mean a lot to me because she gave me my first child. No, that doesn't mean that she is above you. It just means that I'm enjoying having you both around. You running this show, not me, so if you were to cut that shit off today, then that's what it would be."

Leaning over to his side of the car, I voiced, "I love you so much." I placed my lips on his, and he matched my energy by sucking on my bottom lip.

"I can't wait to get you back home," he whispered.

A knock on the window sent me back to my side of the car. It was Star, so I rolled the window down.

"You okay?"

"Yes, I think you should come in here," she said.

"Why would I need to come in there?"

"It's Toya. She's dead."

"Good riddance, shit. Nookie doesn't need to go in there and see that bitch!" Casino spat.

"Chase! She's already dead damn. Don't you think Nookie may want to have some last words or something? I mean, this girl caused her a lot of pain," Star mentioned.

"It wasn't always painful with her, but I am glad that she's gone for good. I mean, even for Bonnie and Micah, she caused them a lot of havoc too. She was a troubled soul. Maybe now she can finally find peace. Bae, I'll just go to see the body to confirm that way I can assure Bonnie that she's gone for good this time." I placed my hand on Casino's knee. I could see in his eyes he was disappointed in the fact that I was going in there, but he'd get over it.

We headed inside and walked through the double doors, and the body was still out. I halted at the door because believe it or not. This would be my first time seeing a dead body. I didn't go to Jason's funeral, nor did I see him get shot months ago so.

"Come on, Nook, she's dead. She won't do anything to hurt you." Star grabbed my hand, and we walked up to the body.

"Wow. Toya is dead. I never thought I'd ever say that. All the times that everybody wanted you dead and I would still talk to you and even planned on meeting you. But, the more you kept showing me that you couldn't respect what I had with Chase, I knew that we'd never work. That's why I had him come to the hotel instead of me. You might've seen it as betrayal, but I saw it as being loyal to the one I loved. We still gave you a chance when we told you to leave again, and it's clear that you didn't. Or maybe you were on the way out of town I don't really know. But, one thing I do know is that you took all the love I ever had for you from me the moment you attacked me. I don't care if you didn't know I was pregnant or not. You still caused me severe harm, and I would've never done that to you. Goodbye, Toya. I hope you find peace, whether it's in heaven or hell. Because your heart was so cold that hell may actually be where you want to be."

I stormed out with tears running down my face.

I didn't know those feelings existed against Toya until I saw that she was never coming back. I was more so crying at the fact that the rest of my pregnancy could be jeopardized based on her actions. I know she was Micah's blood, and now not only did he lose his uncle, but now he lost his cousin as well. I hoped that he'd accept us informing him of her death. I don't know how he'd react because it seemed like their relationship was hot and cold. It'd be okay, though, because I know Bonnie would help him cope.

***

My feet were very swollen due to being in the damn car for so long. I was only four months pregnant, and it seemed like my stomach would poke out a little more every day that went by. Bonnie was released yesterday around four p.m. I honestly think them mafuckas had her waiting longer than she was supposed to. We were planning to surprise them at her place since I still had a key. I just got off the phone with her about an hour ago, and she said she wasn't doing much but catching up on some shows that she'd missed while she was in jail.

We pulled into the driveway and got out of the car. CJ was with my mama for the day, so I knew we were gonna have a good time since nothing had to be censored.

"Baby don't forget the balloons," I told Chase.

"Got 'em. Star, you got the cake?"

"Yes, baby."

The three of us headed to the door, and I pulled out my keys. Once we were inside, I immediately regretted making this a surprise. We done walked in on these mafuckas fucking. Bonnie was riding Micah on the damn couch, and he had a whole titty in his mouth.

"Shit Bonnie! I'm sorry we were trying to surprise you!" I shouted.

"Damn, Nookie! I'm gon' have to get that damn key back." She said as she climbed off Micah.

"Aye, nigga, turn yo ass around!" Micah yelled at Casino as he fixed himself, "Shit, y'all lowkey need to turn around too, y'all got them bisexual vibes and shit."

Laughing hysterically, I yelled, "Shut up, Micah!" I then headed to the kitchen, so we could put the stuff down that we brought in.

By this time, Bonnie had run to the back to get ready, I assumed.

"I think you mafuckas are addicted to sex. Bonnie had already told me y'all ain't waste no time when you brought her home." I snickered.

"She talks too damn much. But, aye it's gon' be even worse once we married. That was just a little quickie, though." Micah chuckled.

"He seduced me," Bonnie said as she came from behind him dressed in a tank top and leggings.

"Lying ass. I had just got out of the damn shower and was walking to the kitchen. Yo ass was the one who started bending over and shit with all that ass. Now, who seduced who?"

We were all cracking up. This the shit I loved the most, just being able to laugh and have a good time with the people who mattered so much to me.

"On to other things, Star, whose body did you have to identify?" Micah asked, looking serious as fuck.

Star looked like a deer in headlights. "Oh, umm, that was umm."

"Spit it out, girl." Bonnie laughed.

"It's probably hard for her to say it because of who it was," I commented.

"Damn, who was it?" Micah pleaded for us to tell him.

"It was Toya," Star said and put her head down.

"Toya?? I wonder what the fuck she was doing in Bloomington. Well, shit, everybody got their time to go." We were sitting there looking crazy as hell for nothing. Micah walked to the freezer and grabbed his bottle of Hennessy out. "Come on, Casino. Let's go play some *2K*."

Chase followed him to the back of the house.

"What is wrong with him?" I asked Bonnie.

"What do you mean? Why in the world would he care about that girl being dead after all the bullshit she put us through?"

"That's still his blood, Bonnie. I thought he'd have a different reaction," Star said.

"Well, he doesn't, so can we talk about something else and not this death shit? Let's talk about why y'all three are together."

"Oh, that?" I repeated.

"Yes, that."

"Shit, whatever it looks like is what it is, Bonnie. I don't really feel like explaining it all. Shit just happened, and it's working out for all of us, especially with seeing CJ all the time, too," I stated.

"Okay, you ain't gotta worry about me saying shit." She laughed, "I'm gonna go talk to them about some business, though. Nookie, I appreciate you for keeping in touch with Micah while I was away."

"Girl, you already know that's my brother-in-law shit, I wouldn't have had it no other way, plus I had to make sure he wasn't about to do something crazy like break you up outta there."

"Shit, I'm surprised he didn't try to. You know he's crazy." Bonnie headed to the back. I looked over at Star and noticed that she wasn't in her element.

"What's wrong?"

"Nothing."

"Star, when we decided to pursue this shit, we all agreed to be honest with one another now what's wrong?"

"I just want to be accepted. Y'all all have a tight ass bond that I want to be a part of."

I grabbed her hands and looked into her eyes, "You are already a part of it. Bonnie will come around, watch. We'll be like the three musketeers. You just have to give it time. As you can see, Bonnie is more of that tough one out of her and me. She's a fighter, and me, I'mma lover."

"Yes, I can definitely tell. Everybody wants them some Nookie."

"Yeah, but everybody can't have the Nookie. They gotta be worth it." I smiled.

"So, I'm worth it?"

Star had me blushing. It was just so easy talking to her.

"Yes, you're definitely worth it." I gave her a sensual kiss and placed my hand in hers.

Some people wouldn't understand the love I had for both sexes. The perfect example was Bonnie. She just didn't comprehend why I would want a woman when a man could balance us women out. It wasn't really meant for Bonnie to understand, but I didn't wanna be judged either.

Chapter 6: Bonnie

I walked into the room that used to be my office, but Micah had turned it into a game room while I was in jail.

"Hey, baby. Wassup?" he asked.

"I gotta talk to y'all. I didn't really want to discuss this with y'all in front of them," I said.

"What's going on?" Casino questioned.

"Which one of y'all killed Toya?"

"Shit, you know I ain't kill my own cousin, I ain't too fucked up about it, but I wouldn't have done that shit."

Casino got quiet.

"Casino?" I scolded.

"I was gon' try to cover it up, but man, y'all ain't even fuck with the bitch like that, so be coo," he said.

"That's not the point. We don't need any damn heat near us right now. Don't you think they'll start following clues and shit?" I whispered harshly.

"Look, Micah, I know that was your cousin, so do what you gotta do. She harmed the mother of my child, what was I supposed to do?" Casino continued to play the game.

Putting the controller down, Micah asked, "How'd you do it?"

Casino put his controller down and answered.

"I ran her off the road. Before that, though, we had offered her money just to leave town. You gave her a chance, and then we did, and she still wanted to just plot against us."

"We can't keep going on like this — no more secrets. From now on, if we have an issue with someone, we bring it to each other. We don't need to keep knocking off mafuckas family members," I expressed.

"You saying that, and it's only my family members that are getting knocked off. I'd be wrong to start doing the same."

"What's that supposed to mean, Micah?"

"I'mma let y'all talk, bro. Are we good?" Casino asked. Micah nodded his head, and then Casino walked out.

"You know what I'm talking about. I've been looking into your father and I'mma find out if he killed my uncle by self-defense or maliciously, and if I find out he had malicious intent, He's gone, Bonnie."

"What the fuck? I thought we already had this discussion, Micah! This is my FATHER. He taught me everything I know, and you want me to be okay with you threatening his life like that?"

Micah was pissing me off. We had already talked about this shit and declared it as self-defense. He would've done the same thing if he was in my father's shoes.

"Bonnie, it ain't a threat. It's a promise. Sleepy was like a father to me. Just because we had a small quarrel doesn't mean I wanted him dead. My loyalty was to him until the day he died."

"Well, your loyalty should be to me now, and I'm asking you to let this go."

Micah and I already had other shit to focus on and worry about. I didn't need for him to bring all this negative energy into shit.

"I'll let it go for now so that we can focus on the wedding and shit, but I do not want him there, Bonnie, and that's that."

"Who's gon' give me away then?"

"We don't need him to give you away shit. Even if he didn't approve, that don't mean shit to me."

"Micah, I'm telling you my father didn't do that shit for no reason!"

"Bonnie."

"If he doesn't come to the wedding, can you just let it go?" I asked.

Micah put the controller on top of the game system and then came over to me, grabbing my hands, "For you, I will do that. I don't have enough to prove anything right now anyway."

"Good, now can we remain in our bliss and focus on what's ahead?"

"Fasho. It's just one more thing I need from you, though."

I saw Micah biting his lip, and I knew what he wanted. He started kissing my neck, and my body instantly shivered. Since I've been home, this nigga's been feening. I didn't care, though, because he had me sprung too. I loved this man with all my heart, and he was so good in the bedroom that I would never be able to let him go.

I closed the door and locked it. I pushed Micah back down into his chair and took off my tank top. I slid out of my leggings as he pulled his dick out his basketball shorts. I was about to ease myself on top of him, but he stopped me.

"What's wrong?" I asked.

"Nah, I wanna eat it first. Put your leg up here," Micah ordered.

He ain't have to tell me twice, if this the way he wanted it, then this was the way he was gon' get it. He was sitting in a rocker game chair so we could make this position work. I placed the sole of my foot on his right shoulder, and he grabbed my leg. Micah started planting kisses all the way up to my inner thigh, which caused me to get chills. I felt his warm breath on my clit before he ran his tongue up and down on it. I leaned my head back in pure ecstasy. This man was truly gifted, and I didn't care if someone else heard me, but I was moaning his name loudly as he moved his tongue faster on my love bud.

"F-fuck babbyyyy, you gon' make me lose my balance," I moaned.

"Don't worry. I promise I got you." In one swift motion, Micah placed my other leg on his other shoulder and palmed my ass in his strong, muscular hands.

He caught me completely off guard, I was trying my best to get my words gathered to curse him out, but the incredible feeling he was giving to me completely took over.

"Right thereeeee! Oh, fuckkkk!" I felt myself explode all over Micah's face, and I just knew his beard was soaked. My legs felt like noodles, and he must've sensed that because he laid me flat on my back on the room floor. He put one of my legs up and ran his dick up and down my pussy lips. Each inch he entered inside of me brought a gasp out of my mouth.

"Fuck, this mafucka so tight. I missed this pussy," Micah groaned as he started stroking me.

"Show me how much," I looked into his eyes and spoke.

There was nothing else that needed to be said after that. Micah bent down, took my right breast in his mouth, and wrapped both of my legs around his waist. After showing my nipples attention, he placed his lips on mines, and we had the most passionate kiss. He started stroking quickly, and my peak was near again. Micah was so selfless when it came to pleasing me. Micah knew the right spots to hit and the pace to go just to get me off multiple times whether it was in an hour or fifteen minutes. I loved me some him.

I bit down on his shoulder to keep from screaming at the top of my lungs. I didn't know if Nookie and them were still in my house, and even though I really didn't care because we were in love, I just didn't trust that Star bitch, so I didn't want her hearing how good Micah put it down. I started matching his pace and gripping his dick while it was inside of me drove him crazy.

"Sssshiiiitttt, slow down," he whispered.

I didn't give a fuck about what he was talking about. I wanted him to cum hard inside of me. I know I've been giving him a hard time about quitting the game, but I wanted to give him the life he wanted. He's been so good to me, so he deserved everything I could give him and more. In a way, we were toxic for each other, but I felt like it was a good type of toxic. Before I knew it, I felt Micah's seeds being released inside of me, and he collapsed on top of me.

"You are something else," he uttered.

"Why you say that?"

"I told you to slow down, and you kept doing that lil move, so I had to bust all inside of that juicy mafucka."

"That's what I wanted you to do." I laughed.

"Oh, so you ready for a baby now?" Micah asked.

"I'm ready to be Mrs. Walker and give you what you want because I love you."

"I love you too. I can't wait to make you my wife." Micah gave me another peck on the lips and slid out.

"You think they gone?" I asked.

"Probably shit, you were screaming loud at first." He chuckled.

"Whatever."

I got up off the floor and opened the door. I didn't hear anything, so I walked out naked and into my bedroom across the hall. Micah followed me.

"So, I was thinking."

"About?"

"When we gon' move in together?"

"Micah, we practically live together. Yo ass ain't ever home." I snickered.

"Yeah, but that ain't official, though. Shit, we can sell my place and put that money towards the wedding."

"I thought that house meant something to you?" I questioned.

"It does, but you mean more, and I want to be around you more and more."

"Hmmm, to spy on me?" I folded my arms across my chest.

"Come on now, you know it ain't even that." He smiled.

"Baby, you turning into a softy on me. It's coo though, I know I got that effect."

"Don't flatter yourself, but you ain't lying, though. You got that good-good, girl."

Laughing hysterically, I voiced, "Yo ass so corny man. But, onto more serious shit, I may have to meet with Miguel myself."

"And why is that?"

"Because, if I'm gon' get out the game, I need to make sure I'm passing it on the right way." I went into the master bathroom and turned the water on.

"And you're thinking about passing it on to Miguel?"

"Who else would I pass everything I do on to?" I wondered.

"Casino."

"Casino? Nah, he's too impulsive."

"Impulsive, how? Shit, he's loyal, and once you're out the game, you don't really have to worry about the shit he does. That'd be on him." Micah followed me into the bathroom.

"Uh, what you think you're doing?" I asked.

"Shit, I'm getting in the shower with you." He laughed.

"Man, hell nah, my pussy's already swollen as fuck." I had a smile on my face, but I was serious.

"Aight then, you be acting like you Tough Tony, but I be breaking yo ass down. Gon' head and tend to Juicy."

"I plan to."

I closed the door behind me and looked in the mirror, but this time I had a smile on my face. Yes, I was facing a case and had to fight to clear my name, but I planned on winning. I had a glamorous wedding to plan. Hopefully, a baby would follow shortly after.

What could possibly go wrong that hasn't already? I've overcome every obstacle that was thrown my way and this case will be next. First thing first, I had to find a way to get Chandlyn off the radar. She practically told me she was going to rat me out just because she wasn't that bitch like I was. Jealousy is a hardcore mafucka and can have people risking it all. Well, I know one thing is for sure, she can try to rat me out all she wants, but it'll be from the grave.

Chapter 7: OG

Crack the sound of Jose's jaw breaking echoed through the old, empty warehouse.

"Mafucka, did you really think that you were safe out here? I see the way you move like as if you can't be touched. You're a snitch, a snake, a bitch ass rat. Did you really think it wasn't gon' catch up with yo ass?" I yelled in his face.

Jose was hardly recognizable anymore. His pale face was now bloody red.

"I-I d-don't know what you talking b-bout," he stuttered.

"Oh, you don't?"

I walked over to my black duffle bag and pulled out a manila folder. Pulling out the pictures from the folder, I started chuckling to myself. This clown was really meeting with the FEDS. He was insulting my intelligence by saying he didn't know what I was talking about, which did nothing but piss me off even more. I lifted one picture. It was the picture of him signing what I would assume was the contract of him becoming an official informant against Diego.

"So, this isn't you?" I asked and watched him avoid the picture altogether. I grabbed the metal bat off the floor and held the picture up again, "Look at this picture is this you or not? And I'd be careful with how you answer it!"

He turned his head to the photo and broke down crying.

"Come on, mannnn! They were going to take me down. I have a familia. Mi abuelo stays with us, so I had to do it. It was hard for me. Diego was like a padre to me." Jose held his head down and sobbed. I just stared at him with disgust in my eyes.

"You sicken me. You said he was like a father to you, and yet you turned him in. There's no place for mafuckas like you on this earth. Sweet dreams."

I held the bat up, and with all my might, I connected the bat with Jose's head as if it were a baseball. You could hear his neck snap in one take. I had planned on this taking hours and hours, but he made me very angry, so I couldn't even look at him anymore. Now that he was out of the picture, I was one step closer to getting rid of anybody who tried to come against my daughter. Once I got him all squared away, I was gon' hit up Mercedes to get my car back, pay her, and head back to Nap.

***

The next morning, I woke up to a knock at my hotel door. I looked through the peephole, and it was Mercedes. Boy, she was looking good as ever. I opened the door and let her walk in just, so I can watch that ass move.

"I hope I was able to assist you as much as I could," she stated in that sexy ass accent.

"You did, I appreciate you very much." I sat on the edge of the bed and stared at her.

"What?" she asked.

"Shit, nothing, my bad. You just so beautiful, but I really need to cool that shit out. I just got out of a bad relationship," I expressed.

"Aww, I'm sorry to hear that. You so sexy and the way you put it down, I'd never mess anything up with you."

"That's what the last female said." I chuckled.

"Well, the last female didn't know what she had then, but I won't hold you up. I just came to collect and bring you your car. I'll be on my way."

"I got you."

I went over to the closet, grabbed the small duffle bag, and handed it to her. She gave me the keys and proceeded to the door.

"Aye," I said.

"Yeah?" She turned around, looking at me.

"If you ever in Nap, just hit me up. I'd love to show you around."

Licking her lips, "I got you, papi." She walked over to me and planted a kiss on my cheek.

"Damn," I said to myself as she dispersed out the door. I shook my head and pinched my dick to make it go down. I showered, packed my shit up, and headed to the airport.

***

I walked out of the airport, expecting to see Bonnie waiting to pick me up because I had just touched back down in Nap, but I didn't see her. I told her last night I would be catching a flight this morning. I pulled out my phone so that I could call her, and that's when I heard my name.

"Aye, OG!" the dude shouted again. I looked up and saw that it was Micah. I headed his direction.

"Wassup? Where's my daughter at?" I questioned.

"She sent me. She thought it would be a perfect time for us to bond or sum shit. Lemme get those bags, pops."

Micah was smiling hard as fuck. Something was off with him. I couldn't put my finger on it, but I planned on finding out real soon. I wasn't aware of any beef, but he ain't ever been this hype to interact with me. I hopped in the passenger seat and waited for him to get back in the truck. It was taking him a little too long just to put some shit in the trunk. I turned my head towards the back, and he was on the phone with somebody. My eyes started roaming all over the truck to find something I could use to protect myself if this mafucka was on one.

"I know this mafucka gotta have some steel in here," I said out loud as I opened the glove department.

I felt underneath my seat and then underneath the driver's seat, and that's when I felt a gun. I saw that it was a .38. I put it in my right hand and placed my arm down, so he wouldn't see it when he got in the truck. Finally, he got in the car and cleared his throat. Once he started driving, it was dead silence. This nigga was on one, and I knew I wasn't tripping. This mafucka must still feel some type of way about his uncle being put in the dirt. I lifted the gun and pointed it to his head.

"Aye, what the fuck wrong with you, man?" Micah yelled.

"What the fuck you up to? It took you forever to get back in the car, and you were on the phone with somebody. I don't trust you, lil nigga."

"Man, you fucking nuts mafucka. Use that mafucka or put the shit away. Bonnie gon' hate yo ass if you do it, though." He had the nerve to chuckle.

"Nigga, you are replaceable, I'm not. She only gets one father. Either say what the fuck you were doing or be laid next to yo uncle, nigga."

Micah started laughing uncontrollably. I didn't get the damn joke.

"I knew it."

"You knew what?" I inquired.

"You killed my uncle because you felt like it. Gon' make up some dumb ass story about self-defense. My uncle wasn't even about that life. There's no way he would've come to you like that." He expressed.

"Yeah, okay. Youngblood, I knew Sleepy well before you knew him. He was jealous of me, and he has always been that way. He was trying to end my life with his bitch of a daughter because she wanted to get back at Bonnie."

I put the gun down and tossed it in the backseat.

"That was like my father, and I'm a man who stands by what the fuck I say. If I find out you killed my uncle over some petty ass bullshit, it's war. He was the only real family I had left. I just found out that Casino's ass killed too my cousin. The difference between you and him though, is that he admitted to doing the shit because she was a threat to the woman he loves. You, on the other hand, your story seemed really shaky, and no one can back you up."

"Do what you gotta do, youngblood. You come into this world with yourself, no one else. Yeah, Sleepy was somebody important to you, but he lived a life outside of you. So, you don't know about everything he was into. You'll learn."

Nothing was left to say. It was dead silence on the way to my house. He dropped me off, and I could barely even get all my bags out the trunk before he sped off.

"Fuck nigga," I said under my breath. For some reason, I had a feeling that someone was burning a hole in my face. Someone was watching me, but who?

Chapter 8: Casino

I took a hit from the blunt as I looked down and watched Nookie bounce her ass back on my dick. I slapped her left ass cheek, leaving my handprint.

"Yesssss, Chaseeee, fuckkkk!" she moaned.

Star grabbed a handful of Nookie's hair as Nookie ate her pussy while I fucked her from the back. Their moans together almost caused me to bust quick as fuck. I pulled out of Nookie and laid flat on my back. I put the blunt in the ashtray on the nightstand, and Star got up and started riding me. Nookie came over to me and started kissing me.

"Put that pussy on my face," I demanded.

My tongue started kissing her clit, and I sucked on it like a juicy peach. She began grinding against my tongue, and I felt her legs shaking. I knew it was only a matter of time before her juices were running down the side of my face. Star bounced up and down on my dick, and I was getting ready to bust.

"Fuckkkk, babbyyyyy! Oh my goddddd!" Star yelled in pure bliss.

I was feeling like the man right now, and nobody couldn't have told me differently. We were all about to reach our climax and at this moment, I was happy as hell that CJ was with Star mama today. After we all released, we laid in the bed. Star and Nookie were cuddled up, and I was spooning Nookie.

"What y'all got planned for the day?" I asked them.

"Nothing really. We were just gon' go to the grocery store and get something for dinner tonight," Star said.

"Nook, you ain't heard from Bonnie?"

Nookie didn't respond, so I nudged her. She was out like a light. This happened every time she busts a nut, especially since she's been pregnant.

"Now, you know she's sleeping." Star laughed.

I could do nothing but laugh. "Shit, I forgot. I should've known. That baby's been having her on her ass."

"You know I've been thinking."

"About?"

"I want another baby."

"Girl, stop playing with me." That was my cue to get up and get ready for the day.

I walked out of the room and headed straight to the bathroom, where I cut the shower on and went back into the bedroom. Star was sitting up with her arms crossed.

"I was serious, Chase."

"I don't care if you were serious or not. We ain't having no more kids." I grabbed my towel and threw it over my shoulder, "You are forgetting something."

"What am I forgetting, Chase?"

"You being around is Nookie's idea, not mine. Of course, I love the fact that I'm around my son a lot, and shit, what nigga don't wanna fuck two females? But this wasn't my idea. After Nookie has this baby, I ain't plan on having no more kids until she ready again."

I was very blunt with Star because I needed her to understand that I will always choose Nookie over her. That's who had my heart. I wasn't in love with Star.

"Wow, Chase. Did you really have to hurt my feelings like that? I don't think I'mma even be able to be around no more!" Star yelled, and I rolled my eyes because she was dramatic as fuck, and I knew she was trying to wake up Nookie.

"That's fine with me, shit. As long as you leave my son."

I didn't say shit else, I just walked out and went to take my shower. I had an important meeting to attend, and I wasn't gon' let Star and her theatrics make me late.

***

When I got out of the shower, Star was gone. I woke Nookie up just to let her know I had somewhere to be and that I would be back. I made up something when she asked me where Star went. I didn't want to upset her either. I was headed to this meeting with what could be my new connect. I didn't feel like Bonnie wanted to share everything she knew with me, and if she planned on quitting the game, I wasn't sure that she'd even let me take over. So, I planned on making some moves myself.

I met this nigga named Tek while I was playing ball the other day. Come to find out we both used to work for Amazon when I was legit a couple of years ago. Once I found out how to make fast money, I never went the legal way and didn't plan to. He said he knew somebody in his family that had major connections to some high-quality dope, and I jumped on that shit ASAP. I needed to know how to be a part of it.

The location was about thirty minutes out. He said they lived in Greenwood in the subdivision Brighton Estates, right past Greenwood Mall. I felt like it was a little weird that they'd invite me to their home without even knowing me, but that just made me see that they must've been powerful enough to protect themselves.

I reached my destination and parked on the curb of the home. They were in a cul-de-sac, so it wasn't too many cars outside. I walked up to the door and rang the doorbell. I stood there for about five minutes, and right before I was about to walk off, the door opened. It was a big nigga that stood about 6'6 and had to weigh like 350 pounds.

"She's expecting you." His deep voice had my eyes big as fuck.

I wasn't scared of nobody, but this nigga looked twice the size of Mark Henry type shit. What the fuck he meant SHE's expecting me? Goddamn, are we in a new day and age where bitches really run shit? This shit is getting outta hand.

I followed him through the hallway of the house that I assumed lead to the bedroom and shit. On the way to wherever he was leading me, my eyes wandered, and I saw that this mafucka wasn't a house at all. It was a damn trap house. Along the way, I could see bitches bagging up dope, and in one room, they were counting hella money. This mafucka got a trap house right in the middle of Greenwood, Indiana. I guess it makes sense, though, because they would never think that something was going on like this by how the outside of the house looks.

We reached the main room, and he knocked twice before entering. It was a big ass office setup.

"Have a seat. She'll be right out," the dude said before walking out and closing the door.

"What the fuck?" I whispered to myself. I was about to call Tek because I wanted to know what the fuck he was about to get me into, and I honestly thought his ass was gon' be here. Before I was about to dial his number, a door inside the room opened, and there she was. She was beautiful, no doubt, if I weren't all for Nookie, I'd probably have this bitch bent over by tonight.

"Did you need to call someone?" she asked.

"Nah, I'm good now. I was just gonna hit Tek up and see why he wasn't around," I explained.

"Well, that's because he doesn't need to be. He told me you were looking to become the next big thing when it comes to this line of business." She sat in the chair across from me and crossed her legs.

"I did say that, but not in those words. He knows I'm already established in this business, and I may even have a chance at taking over in the next couple of months."

"Why do you feel the need to wait?"

"Because the person who runs it hasn't stepped down yet."

"Who? Bonnie?" I was shocked that she knew who I was working under.

"How'd you know that? I never told Tek who I was working with," I stated.

"For. You mean who you are working for. From what I heard, Bonnie pretty much runs shit. I have to salute her, though, because you don't always see a woman in her position."

"But, aren't you in her position?"

"Nope, she wishes she were in my position, I'm a very important person, and we are all very much connected. However, she's starting to get sloppy. She was almost killed, and so were the people around her. She doesn't have enough security to continue to be in a position of power. I ran some numbers, and it looks to be that you make the most money out of her runners. So, how would you feel about replacing her?"

"Who are you?" I asked.

"I'm Laina Rodriguez, Diego's wife."

Chapter 9: Bonnie

"You sure you can do this without causing attention?" I asked one of my runners who had a reputation for shooting first and asking questions later.

We were meeting in Eagledale Plaza at Sakitumi Liquor Store. I was supposed to be on my way to meet the wedding planner with Micah. He was just gon' meet me there at her office.

"Yes, they don't call me Sniper for nothing. Nobody will hear a thing. My cousin works there, so he plans on getting me inside," he conveyed.

"Aight coo. I'm not tryna get my hands dirty with this shit while the case is going on. You see anything tricky, and you get out of there ASAP." I ordered.

"I got you, Bonnie. You ain't gotta worry about shit. You showed me a picture of her, I sent it to my cousin, and he told me which cell she was in. Unfortunately for her, he works the night shift, so she's fucked."

"Bet. Hit me up when it's done. I'll make sure we got an alibi straight for you just in case."

"Coo," Sniper said and then walked off.

I walked into the liquor store to grab me a fifth of Rémy. I just wanted to make sure I had one more drink just in case I turned out to be pregnant. The way Micah busted up in me the last time we had sex, I was sure that I'd be pregnant sooner than later.

"Hey, sexy, what's your name?" I rolled my eyes as the older man came at me.

"Minding my business. That's my name, I said as I walked around him to get to the cashier.

"Aww, you a stuck-up bitch, huh?"

The man was yelling. He came from the other side of the liquor store where the bar was and was already drunk. I looked at my phone, and it was only three p.m.

"Watch your mouth when you're talking to me. You must not know who I am." I stared at him.

"Fuck you, bitch!" he spat. When he turned around, a bottle went up against his head. I was happy somebody shut him up. It was my daddy.

"Daddy, what are you doing here?" I went and hugged him.

"I should be asking you that. You ain't been on this side of town in quite some time. Aye," he said to the cashier, "you might wanna get somebody to get this mafucka off the floor."

He paid for my stuff, and then we walked out.

"So, why did Micah pick me up and not you when I got back from the airport?"

"He offered to do it. Shoot, I was tired." We went over to my car, and I placed the bottle in the trunk.

"Well, you were almost a widow before you even got married. This mufucka is still salty about his punk ass uncle."

"Daddy, don't even be doing all that. You know you'd be shitty too if you KNEW who killed a family member and had to deal with that mafucka being around."

"Watch ya mouth." He glared at me.

"Sorry, but you get what I'm saying. I'm your daughter, and he's my fiancé. Like he literally can't get rid of someone that got rid of somebody that practically raised him," I explained.

"Don't get me wrong. I get it. I really do. But, how he gon' have that energy towards me and not towards Casino's ass, and he offed his cousin?"

"I have no idea why he let that go so easily. I mean, I guess I could say it's because she was a problem for EVERYBODY. Sleepy rarely fucked with anyone."

"True, but, like I told him, I wasn't about to not defend myself. Sleepy's daughter was with another female that night. I'mma try to find her, and when I do, she will vouch for me that they had a plan to come at me."

"I got you. I'm trying my best to keep the drama down, but as of now, he doesn't want you at the wedding."

"So, my only daughter is getting married, and I can't even give her away?"

My daddy looked so hurt, and that broke my heart. I had to fix this shit because I wanted my father to give me away. I didn't wanna go against Micah, but he would have to understand. I would have to conjure up a plan to get them on one accord.

"I'll talk to him," I told him before climbing into the car.

"Wait, have you talked to Nookie? How's she been, and is the baby okay?"

"Yes, I think the baby is okay. She's supposed to find out what she's having, and if the placenta is still intact. I haven't talked to her in a couple of days, though."

"Well, just keep me posted on everything. I got some moves to make. I need to talk to you about something I had to take care of, but this ain't the place. Maybe I'll swing by later when you're alone, and Micah ain't around."

"Daddy, don't be like that. Now, I gotta go meet the wedding planner. Love you!"

"Love you too, baby girl." He closed my door and watched me pull off.

I felt like a teenager again bringing my boyfriend over for my father's approval. I was in a completely different place than when I first met Micah. Then, I took shit from nobody, feelings barely existed, and now that I'm about to be a wife, I feel all these different types of emotions, which is not bad, but I don't wanna feel like I'm not that bitch anymore. I loved it when people were afraid to cross me or come at me reckless. Now, people were getting out they body and believed they could even speak to me. That shit had to come to an end.

Nookie was living her best life with her three-way relationship. I wish I would've known how much of a nympho she was, I would've been seen the crazy shit that came along. I was worried, though, because our friendship seemed to be disappearing day by day. This Star bitch just came and damn near replaced me all because she can please Nookie in a way that I'd never be interested in doing. It was coo, though, because if the friendship is real, it'll always come back to normal.

***

"There she is!" my wedding planner Jane said as she got up out of the chair to hug me.

"Hey, Ms. Jane, how are you doing? It's been forever since I saw you."

"It surely has. Does your father know I'm planning your wedding?"

"No, that's a part of the surprise for him. He doesn't know I'm using the person who planned him and my mama's wedding. Speaking of, do you remember the dress she had at the wedding?"

"Yes, how could I forget it? It was custom made just for her. The smile on her face when she saw it is embedded in my mind."

"You gon' make me cry, Ms. Jane, but I want that same dress concept. That's the second part of the surprise for him."

"Aww, Bonnie. That's so amazing. I'd be honored to get it done. You know the designer is a close friend of mine. She's still in the business."

"Thank you so much!" I hugged her again.

I was happy we got this part of the conversation out of the way. Right on cue, Micah walked in. He didn't know that my daddy was attending the wedding, whether he liked it or not, so I did not want to talk about this in front of him.

"Sorry, I'm late." He kissed me on my cheek.

"It's okay, baby."

"Let's get started. Micah, I'm Jane, it's nice to meet you. I've known Bonnie since she was a little girl."

"Nice to meet you too."

Micah's attitude was off, and I was wondering if everything was okay, but we'd deal with that after we leave from here.

"Okay, what type of budget were you guys looking at?"

"It's 50K," Micah said.

My eyes got big. I didn't even think he was gon' say that amount. I was thinking 25K, but I had no complaints. That just meant my wedding was gon' be nice as hell.

"Well, first things first, do you have the bridesmaids and groomsmen squared away?" Jane asked.

"I mean, I barely have any female friends any damn way, so it won't be many," I stated.

"Well, maybe if you just had a maid of honor and Micah, you'd have a best man," Jane suggested.

"What you think, bae?" I turned to him.

Nonchalantly speaking, he voiced, "That's coo."

"Jane, may we have a moment alone, please? I just need to speak to my fiancé."

"Sure thing, I'll go grab some wedding books so that we can pick out a theme." She got up and went to the back of the office.

"What's going on now, Micah?"

"What do you mean?"

"I mean you honestly looking like you don't wanna be here right now. Do you still wanna get married?" He was making me very frustrated because he was the reason that I was even going through with this shit. He knew how I felt about being locked down and shit.

"Bonnie, you know I wanna get married. I just told you that shit the other day. It's just a lot on my mind."

"Like what?"

"Shit, like how? Ever since we've been together, my life's really got placed on the backburner and now my mafuckin' family is dropping like flies." There was venom laced with his words and I didn't understand why it all was coming out now.

"And mine didn't, Micah? I think BOTH of our lives have been altered because we decided to be together. Just like you itching to get out there and blow a mafucka head off, I'm itching to make pop-ups at the warehouses, count some weight, pick up the drops. But I slowed all that shit down because YOU said you wanted a wife and not a queen pin."

"I never said it in those exact words."

"You practically did."

"Lower your voice, Bonnie. It doesn't even have to be all that, and you just talking freely like that lady can't hear us."

"Oh, please, Micah. She threw the wedding for my mama and daddy, so she's been around for years. She already knows how we get down."

I was very annoyed. Micah had me messed up, trying to say that his life has changed drastically and all that shit. All our lives changed the moment we laid eyes on each other.

"Maybe I just need a way to release some frustration," he said and sat back in his chair.

"I bet, and what's the real reason you offered to go pick my daddy up from the airport?"

"I wanted to confront him about my uncle."

"After we already talked about it over and over again."

"I don't give a fuck. What if the roles were reversed? You would be on the same shit."

Micah made a good point. I mean I knew it was hard for him to be with me dealing with that. I had a plan to get they asses on the same page, though, because this was very annoying. I just was ready to change subjects. I called Jane back out, and we decided to go with the Classic Glamourous theme with the colors gold and white. We'd have the wedding this upcoming fall. Once we were finished, we walked out of the office in separate directions. I didn't know if Micah was just getting cold feet or what issues he had going on.

However, I had an idea that would help him, and my father let out some built-up frustration.

***

It had been two days since we met with the wedding planner, and we hardly said two words to one another. Micah stayed at the house that he was supposed to be selling. I couldn't lie. I was nervous that he was having second thoughts, but I believed in everyone getting time to themselves. I just assumed that he needed to think about if he wants this or not. After I woke up this morning, I refused to let another day go by without us being under one roof. So, I texted him and my daddy and told them to meet me around one p.m. at the Sarkine's Total Warrior boxing gym off West Washington Street. I rented it out for an hour so that no one saw what was going to take place. There were no cameras or anything like that.

It was currently 12:59 p.m., and nobody walked in yet. I was anxious to see who would be the first to arrive. I pulled my phone out of my pocket and there were no new notifications.

"Man, what the hell?" I mumbled under my breath.

I was getting ready to call Micah, but then I heard the doors open. I heard arguing, and I rolled my eyes.

"Nah, because you a sneaky mufucka. And I can't be beefing with my damn girl because she got a snake ass father."

"Lil nigga, I will body yo ass right the fuck here. Don't get shit twisted. Bonnie is literally the ONLY reason yo blood ain't splattered on the ground," I heard my father say.

My eyes got big as I ran over to meet them.

"Ayyyeeeee, calm that shit down! What is wrong with y'all?" I shouted.

"Bonnie, what the fuck are we doing here? Why would you invite me anywhere this mafucka is at?" Micah questioned me.

"Because y'all wanna keep on having this pissing match with one another, fight the shit out. It's boxing gloves in the ring. This killing shit is dead. We cannot have any more murders anywhere near us. If the FEDS connects the dots, it's over for me," I explained.

"Bonnie, I'm not doing no childish ass boxing match," my daddy said.

"Then what you gon' do?! Kill 'em? Go right ahead," I said.

"He ain't gon' do shit." Micah glared at him.

"Nah, y'all gon' head and shoot it out then. Because what y'all don't realize is if either one of you harms the other, I'm done with that mafuckin' person, period. So, it's a lose-lose situation. Y'all rather kill each other or knock each other off, and then y'all still gon' lose me during that."

"What is this supposed to do, though? Because once I beat his ass, he gon' be salty, and you might be too for me fucking yo daddy up."

"Fuck who up? Man, let's get this shit started, this lil nigga don't know who the fuck he dealing with."

I watched my daddy walk towards the ring and Micah followed, but then he stopped dead in his tracks.

"Ain't you coming?" He asked me.

"Nah, y'all do what y'all gotta do, I'mma go try to meet up with Nookie to catch up with her. Byeeeee."

I laughed as I walked away. They needed to figure this shit out and fast because I was getting sick and tired of it. For now, I was gon' go check on Nookie and my god baby.

Chapter 10: Micah

I was getting ready to knock this mafucka's teeth out. I grabbed the red gloves leaving him with the blue ones.

"Now, you know you saw me go for the red ones," OG said.

"I don't give a fuck. This is my favorite color, get them blue ones, whack ass crip." I chuckled.

"You got me fucked up. Matter a fact fuck the gloves. Let's go hands up."

"Quickest way to break yo jaw, say less," I threw the gloves to the side and squared up.

We were about the same in height, so I knew my hits were gon' land. We both were waiting on the other to bust a move. Finally, he swung on me, and I ducked and placed a two-piece to his ribs.

"Arggghh!" he shouted in frustration and then hit me with a nice left, which connected with my jaw.

Blood filled my mouth, and that really pissed me off. This mafucka had me leaking already, and the fact that he had me shedding blood FIRST, made me very angry. I spit the blood on the floor of the ring.

"Damn youngblood, you ain't expect that, did you?" He chuckled.

"Fuck you."

We were jumping around the ring, wondering who was gon' make their next move. Then, without warning, this mafucka damn near speared my ass like we were in a wrestling match. He hit me once in my jaw, and I threw punches on his back and started elbowing him in his spine. He fell to the ground, and before I could gain control, he did a flip to get back on his feet. He made the mistake of leaving his face unblocked, so I punched him in the nose and blood flew out. While he was holding his nose, I saw that this was my chance. I put him in a headlock and could hear him breathing hard as fuck.

"Now what? What was all that tough Tony talk, OG?" Every ounce of strength I had was going into trying to pop his head off his shoulders.

"L-Let me go, mufucka," he uttered.

"Nah, let's end this shit right here and now."

"Is th-this what you want? You want Bonnie to hate you forever?" He mustered up enough energy to say that.

I thought about what decision to make, and it was a hard one. I released him and hopped on my feet just in case he thought of retaliating. He started coughing uncontrollably, and I just stood there looking on, massaging my jaw.

"You can thank Bonnie that I didn't just end your life just now. I want no dealings with you, mafucka. I don't want you anywhere near me or anything I got going on, and that includes the fucking wedding. I beat yo ass, so I don't need to do shit else, and we don't ever have to cross paths."

"Nigga, I let you win. That's what's wrong with you, young niggas, y'all too impulsive. However, I do know it's a hard pill to swallow when someone close to you is taken away. I understand how you feel completely." OG was talking as he got up and straightened his shirt out. He wiped the blood coming out his nose with the back of his hand. "BUT, there's one thing you WILL understand mafucka, I'm walking my daughter down that aisle. If you got a problem with that, then you can find you somebody else to marry."

We were face-to-face as if we were in a boxing match forreal. I was over the shit and tired of being angry when shit wasn't gon' change. I ain't have to fuck with this nigga on a day-to-day basis.

"Just stay the fuck out my way before you be buried next," I said through clenched teeth and got out the ring. That nigga would have his day coming sooner or later. I was just gon' let the shit play out.

***

I regretted the dumb ass fight Bonnie had set up the previous morning, I woke up sore as fuck from the shit, and my hand was swollen. It was coo, though, because I knew OG was hurting worse than I was. I looked over at Bonnie sleeping and wondered if I could put my pride to the side for her. I made it up in my mind right then and there that I could. I loved her so much, and she turned me from a player to a one-woman man. Only two women could say they did that to me. Bebe's crazy ass damn near didn't count though, especially after that shit she pulled a couple of months ago with Bonnie's piece of shit father.

What Bonnie didn't know is I had big plans for us, major plans. She probably was still irritated with my big blow up I had when we were visiting the wedding planner. But, truth be told, I know she doesn't just want my business to take the backseat, she's always been a big fan of making money from all angles. Shit, when she was assigning the hits after she got shot, she made a lot of revenue.

I guess she felt me staring at her because she started stirring in her sleep.

"Why are you staring at me, Micah? You know I hate that."

She rolled over on her other side.

"Man, stop playing, turn back to me."

She rolled back over and rolled her eyes at me.

"I'mma beat you up," she said.

"You gon' beat me up after I had to beat ya daddy up?" I was cracking up.

"I told you I ain't wanna know the results of that shit."

"Why? You the one who suggested it happen."

"Yeah, because y'all don't know how to let stuff go. I'm not going another day wondering if my daddy gon' kill my fiancé or vice versa. I thought men didn't hold grudges?"

"I hear you. I put that shit to rest. If he stays away from me, and we don't cross paths, I believe it could be good for all of us," I explained.

"Whatever you say, Micah. I got to talk to you about something, though." She sat up, and we both had our backs against the headboard of the bed.

"What's wrong?"

"Nothing is really wrong. I just wanted to make sure I share everything I have going on with you to keep you in the loop. So, remember when the judge said I could get out on bail, they sent me back to the holding cell, right?"

"Right."

"Well, guess who was in fucking jail too and had court the same day?" I just looked and wondered who it was. "Chandlyn, it's like this bitch will never go away unless I make her go away."

"What do you mean make her go away? How you gon' do that if she locked up?"

"I got my ways. I just needed you to know that it's happening. I don't want to hide anything from you because if it gets tied back to me, you'd at least know. I mean, I doubt that it would happen."

I took everything she was saying in and got frustrated. I didn't give a fuck about Chandlyn at all, but it was the fact that she had to participate in some more bullshit that could risk her freedom.

"Look, we need to discuss when you getting up outta this shit. That's just something more that we have to be worried about if the mafucka you utilizing turn FED, which has been a major factor in all the bullshit we've endured for the last six months. You're trusting mafuckas who have hidden agendas."

"Don't you think I know that, Micah? Damn, like I don't need you constantly reminding me of that shit. I have my own plans on my own time, and you and whoever else not gon' rush me about it."

She got out the bed and stormed into the bathroom. I followed her ass.

"Damn, can I use the bathroom in peace?" she asked, annoyed as hell.

"That shit's dead, especially now that I'm moving in." I chuckled.

"Oh, now you moving in, you said that last week, got mad at me, and stayed there for two days."

"So, you don't know why I was staying there so hush up."

"Why is it always an argument or debate with us? Like when we're playing or on some freaky shit, it's coo, but that shit gets annoying when it's at random ass times like now or when I just woke up."

"I apologize, you're right. We gon' work on that shit."

"Good." Bonnie got herself together and then flushed the toilet. After washing her hands, she came over to me and placed her arms around my neck.

"I have a meeting with Miguel. He supposed to be coming down here. His plane arrives around six p.m. tonight."

"That's coo. I'm sure we should be able to wrap up everything with him."

"We?"

"Yes, *we*. You think I'mma let you round that nigga without me being there?"

"LET?"

"Yes, LET."

"Okay, massa."

"Whatever, you love when I talk to you like that, so dead the act." Bonnie started cracking up, and I kissed the corner of her mouth, "Yeah, you know I love yo ass, cause that breath is tart."

We started laughing hysterically. Bonnie might've thought I was joking, but I wasn't playing with her ass. I'm going to that damn meeting just to make sure she discussed quitting the game.

Chapter 11: Sniper

I was hype as fuck when Bonnie told me she wanted me to complete a mission for her. Nobody knows how long I've been trying to even get noticed. Do you know how it feels to be making money for someone, and they don't even know that you're there? That's how I fucking felt. Bonnie used to be knee deep into this dope game shit, but now since she gets her back broke on the regular. She's slowly starting not to give a fuck about this shit no more. I wasn't mad, though, because that just meant I'd have a chance at standing out. If she saw that I was willing to put in more work just to get her attention, she'd want to hand over everything to me.

I was getting ready to eliminate someone who made the dumb ass decision to expose themselves as a rat to Bonnie dead in her face. It was some light-skinned broad named Chandlyn. My cousin had left one of the exits unlocked, so I would be able to enter the jail without being seen. Everybody knows that in jail there's usually no way to escape unless they make a way. She did have a cellmate, though, and I was worried about that until my cousin said he'd move her to another cell for a small fee. It worked out perfectly because he waited until she was asleep to move the other cellmate. He left the cell open just a little so that it looked like it wasn't open at all.

I arrived in front of the cell that she was in and saw her sound asleep in the bed. I pulled out my phone and texted my cousin, letting him know I was here so that way he knew not to come down the hall.

Quietly walking in, I slowly walked over to her and some thoughts ran through my mind while staring at her. Her body was banging, and she was a beautiful ass girl. Maybe I'd have some fun with her before I did what Bonnie ordered me to do. I grabbed the chloroform and the rag out of my duffle bag that I held in my right hand. When I turned back around, she was looking at me with fear in her eyes. Before she could scream, I grabbed her neck extra tight and placed the rag over her face. When she lost consciousness, I threw her over my shoulder and closed the cell back. Swiftly, I took her to my car and put her in the trunk. I text my cousin telling him I was done and got the fuck out of dodge.

***

My palms were sweating, I fucked up by not leaving her dead in the cell. I know Bonnie expected to see pictures of the job done, but once I pulled off, more ideas started coming to my head. What if I could keep her as leverage for protection for myself? If Bonnie doesn't give me a higher position, I can lure this bitch over her head in exchange for more power. I'd have some fun along the way, though, because she was looking right in that orange jumpsuit. That mafucka couldn't hide her body shape if it wanted to. I sat in a folded chair across from her as she laid on the floor stirring. She was getting ready to come to. I had her tied up with zip ties just in case she tried to run. She jumped up and started screaming.

"HELPPP!!! SOMEBODY HELP ME, PLEASE!!!!!"

"No one can hear you," I said calmly.

"Who the fuck are you? You work for Bonnie, don't you?"

I clenched my jaw. I hated when mafuckas said that shit. "I'm an associate of Bonnie's. What did you do for her to want you dead?"

"Why should I talk to you?" she asked.

"Because your life is in my hands now. You either cooperate with me, or I'll deliver your head to her tomorrow on a silver platter." I smirked at her, and immediately tears started falling down her face. "Stop all that crying, how did you last in jail when you can cry at the drop of a dime? Develop some thicker skin."

Sniffing, she asked, "What do you mean?"

"Shit, you fine as fuck. I wouldn't mind having you on my arm. A situation that was intended for a bad outcome can turn into something good, but I'm not about to have a soft ass bitch on my arm, even if it's for play purposes only."

"And how would I be arm candy when I was just locked up in jail? I'm sure they gon' be looking for me. Bonnie gon' be looking for me too since I threatened to turn her in," Chandlyn spoke in an annoyed manner.

"How about you let me worry about all that? My cousin works there. You think they gon' give a fuck about a missing inmate. They got bigger fish to fry like Bonnie."

"Well, if you a man of your word and you promise to protect me, I have no problem being by your side. You look good yourself. It's just a shame we had to meet under these circumstances. I'm sure we can grow to like each other."

We had a stare down, and I pondered on the words she said to me.

"I ain't no rat so that ratting idea you had. You need to get that up out yo mind if you rocking with me. Yeah, the FEDS might want Bonnie in custody, but it won't be because of me or the person I'm fuckin' wit."

"You have my word. If you put me in a position where I can gain power and mean something, I'll do whatever you say. Please take these off." She held her wrists up in the air, so I could cut the zip ties.

I smiled big as fuck because this bitch was a groupie and clearly just wanted some attention. It's coo, though. Ain't nothing wrong with getting some good pussy on top of making this money too. I was only gon' use this bitch for everything she knew about Bonnie. I was ready to start making big moves, and if Bonnie didn't see how good I was, I'd make her see. Once it got to that point, there's no more working for any damn body. My new title would be public enemy #1 from then on.

Chapter 12: Nookie

I was tired as hell when I got home. It was a long day at the shop. Star was acting weird all damn day and giving me dry ass responses. I didn't know what was wrong with her. I just said fuck it. Maybe Chase said something to rub her the wrong way. He does that often.

After putting my stuff down on the counter, I looked in the freezer and rolled my eyes. I was all out of a Rocky Road ice cream, and that pissed me off because I made it very well-known how much I loved that ice cream, and it was one of the few things this damn kid in my belly would let me eat without throwing shit up. I picked up my phone to call Chase to ask him to get me some more. That was until I heard the door opened, and he rushed in, slamming the door behind him.

"Baby, what's wrong?" I questioned.

"Man, I just got like the offer of a lifetime!" He came over to me and picked me up, spinning me in a circle.

"OMG! Put me down! I'mma throw up on you!" I laughed as he put me back down on my feet, "Tell me!"

"You know Diego, right? He's the one who was the original connect before somebody ratted him out. His wife set up a meeting between me and her through her nephew. Apparently, she knows all about what's been going on with Bonnie, her daddy, and all that shit. She wants me to take over Bonnie's position."

Chase was so excited, and I just looked at him, confused because I know he didn't think we were going to go to war with my best friend.

"What's wrong with you? Do you know what this means for us?"

"Chase, I don't care. We are not stepping on my best friend's toes. She's been doing this shit for how long now?"

"Nookie, here we go. It's not personal. Shit, Micah wants her out of the game anyway." He plopped on the couch and started taking his shoes off.

"Chase, I don't give a damn what Micah wants. He ain't her damn daddy, and even if her daddy wanted her to quit, she wouldn't. She will when she good and damn ready."

"Aight now Nookie, you making this shit about girl power and all that shit. This is about our safety and handling this shit right so that we can be comfortable for our kids. Bonnie's got a lot of heat on her right now, and it's not good for business."

"I don't care. Tell the bitch the answer is no," I said as I walked to the back of the house.

I couldn't believe this shit. I was getting ready to call Bonnie and let her know because Lord knows if I don't and she hears it elsewhere, I ain't gon' hear the end of it."

I grabbed my phone off the nightstand and noticed that Star didn't respond to my last message. I dialed Bonnie and waited for her to pick up the phone. Chase walked in, saw that I was on the phone, threw his hands up in the air, and walked back out. I rolled my eyes at him.

"Hello?"

"Hey, boo, what you doing?"

"Girl, nothing, looking at these wedding books, I'm tryna figure out like what type of flowers and stuff to get."

"About that, why haven't you asked me for any help with your wedding?"

She just got silent, and I was getting irritated.

"Because."

"Because what?"

"You have a lot going on with the baby and all that. You're still my maid of honor."

"Nah, you just don't want nobody giving you no input on your wedding. It's not even supposed to be about that. This is a huge milestone in your life, and you should want your best friend by your side."

"You right, I should've personally invited you to help me with my wedding."

"You are being sarcastic.

"I am not."

"Yes, you are, but onto serious things."

"Damn, please don't tell me it's something with the baby?"

"No, no, it's not that. So, Chase came home excited as fuck, right. I'm like what's going on. This nigga's talking about Diego's wife set up a meeting with him asking him to take over your organization."

"I know you lying."

"No, I'm dead ass. I told him that that's an absolute NO. Like, how is she gon' try to get y'all against each other."

"Where the fuck she even come from, and who the fuck does she think she is? She can't dictate shit I got going on. I don't give a fuck if she's married to Diego or not. That nigga is locked up for the rest of his life. I'mma get down to the bottom of this shit. Thanks, Nook."

I heard the sadness in her voice, and it probably was because shit changed so much from how it was last year. It was so bittersweet. We both came from loneliness and found two men that loved us unconditionally, but we didn't expect shit to change so much. She was so used to being that bitch that made her own decisions and the one to hold her ground. Everybody used to know not to fuck with Bonnie, and now it's like she was looked at as a joke since she got shot. In my eyes, she was the strongest woman I know, and I don't see why people didn't take her serious anymore. All I knew was that I wanted her to quit, not because she didn't know how to do what she does, but because I want her to stay alive. But, I'd be damn if she was gon' get out that game because a man wanted her to.

"Bonnie, I'm sorry. I just felt like you needed to know as soon as possible so that you'd know what to do to prepare yourself."

"I appreciate it. You know I'm getting a little overwhelmed. My life was so different last year. I don't know how much longer I can take this shit. It's like I got people coming at me from all angles. And what I'm starting to see, but afraid to admit, is that ever since I met Micah, shit been going downhill for me.

"I just think it's because you're having a hard time balancing out everything. I mean, before Micah came around, all you had to worry about was your organization, not love. So, now that love is a part of your life, you have to balance everything out and not confuse one with the other."

"You're right. Look at you over here schooling me on life and shit." Bonnie laughed.

"You already know. I just wanted to give you a heads up just in case some fuck shit goes down. And to let you know that I'm not a part of that shit."

"I mean Nook you kinda are. Casino's basically telling you he's gon' go against me, and you're still gonna be there."

"Bonnie, what you want me to do? I love him, and he's the father of my child. I can't just drop him because of some game y'all playing."

"It's not a game, Nookie. People die in this so-called game, but say less."

This bitch hung up after that.

I stared at my phone, just shaking my head. *Did she really threaten my nigga's life?* This shit is insane, and I honestly did not have the time for it. I needed to put all my focus on my unborn child and decide when I was gon' take off from work. My clients are already giving me an earful because they don't wanna go to anyone else. I know one thing was for sure, I was gon' make sure we all sat and talked this shit out. Whoever this bitch Laina is, she's trying to mess with my family, and I'm not going for it.

***

It was finally time to find out what I was having, and I was excited and nervous at the same time. I'm always nervous, whether it's just a regular check-up for me or a heartbeat check for the baby. Ever since that bitch Toya did that shit to me, I've been worried that I will get bad news every time we go in.

Chase and I were waiting in the exam room and the vibe was slightly off. He was pissed that I told Bonnie about Laina offering him her spot. I just felt that she couldn't do that. I don't care who her husband is. That mafucka's locked up and shouldn't be trying to make any changes from the inside if it was his idea.

I thought I'd break the ice while we waited for the doctor to step in.

"Did you see Star at all today?" I asked.

"Nah," Chase responded drily as hell.

"Okay, what about CJ? Star's been acting a little weird. She has returned none of my calls since we were texting yesterday."

"Maybe it's because she told me she wanted me to give her another baby, and I told her hell no since I'm with you. That's what loyalty looks like."

"Loyalty? So, I'm not loyal because I told my best friend for over ten years that people were plotting against her? So, loyalty doesn't matter unless it pertains to you?" I questioned.

"I ain't say all that, but I'm the nigga you sleep with every night. I'm the father of your child. There gotta be some type of line you just don't cross."

He was pissing me off. Before I had a chance to rebuttal, the doctor walked in.

"Good morning Nachelle, how are you doing today?" The doctor was smiling big as hell.

"Hi, Dr. Graham, I'm fine."

"Well, you don't sound too excited about the big day. We find out what the baby is! Is this dad?"

"Yes, he was busy with work at my first couple of appointments. That's why you're just now meeting him," I explained.

"How are you doing today, sir?" the doctor asked Chase. He put on a front smiling big as hell like he just wasn't cursing me out five minutes ago.

"I'm fine, ma'am, just ready to see what my baby is."

"I won't hold you guys off then. Let's get started."

I pulled my shirt up and leaned back on to the exam table. She came over with the ultrasound machine. After she put gloves on and placed the gel on my belly, she took the probe and moved around on my stomach. I watched her facial expressions as she started going in circles.

"What's wrong, doctor?"

Clearing throat, she voiced, "This is not technically a bad thing unless you all don't want this. It could be a good thing," she stated.

"Aight doc, you beating around the bush." Chase was getting irritated.

"There's more than one child in your belly," she admitted.

"How many more?" I yelled.

"Two."

"Oh, so I'm having twins?!" I shouted excitedly.

"No, I'm sorry, maybe I phrased that wrong. You're having TWO additional kids on top of the one that's in your belly."

"Wowwwww, so I'm having triplets?! Chase, I'm having triplets, I think I'm about to hyperventilate." I panicked. He rushed over to me and grabbed my hand.

"Calm down, baby."

Chase started massaging my hand, and this is exactly why I loved him. Just his touch could make me relax. Even though he was mad at me right now, he didn't let it take over his feelings for me. He always made sure I was good, mad or not.

"I'm sorry, Nachelle, the other embryos tend to be more noticeable once time goes on within the pregnancy. If you want to know, I could tell you what they are. I already checked, and they are all flaunting what they have in between their legs." The doctor smiled.

"OMG, so you telling me I'm having three more sons?" Chase was ecstatic, and it made me even happier just by watching his reaction. I knew he was gon' be a great dad to our sons right along with CJ.

"Man, I so wanted a girl." I was sad because I wanted to have a little mini-me running around.

"You will," the doctor said.

"What do you mean? I thought they were all boys," Chase asked.

"They are all flaunting what they have in between their legs, but one of them is a girl. So, Nachelle, you'll be having two baby boys and a baby girl." The doctor smiled.

"Oh, I'm sorry for gloating baby, but at least you got your girl." He kissed my forehead, "I'm not too excited, though, because now I gotta kill any little boy that thinks he's gon' mack on her."

"Well, that depends on how good this delivery goes shoot." I chuckled.

"Uh-oh," the doctor said.

"Uh-oh, what? What's going on?" My heart was beating so fast. All I knew is this shit better not be horrible news.

"The placenta is having a hard time staying intact, have you been bleeding?" she asked me.

"No, not really, I think I noticed like two spots of blood when I went to the restroom one time, but that's it."

"We'll monitor it very closely. If it gets worse than this, Nachelle, you'll be on bed rest at this hospital until it's time for those babies to come out, and that's for your safety and theirs. Do you all have any other questions?"

She took the probe off and gave us the few pics she took. She grabbed a towel and wiped off the gel.

"No doctor, I guess we'll just have to take it easy," Chase said.

"Yes, the best thing right now would be no strenuous activity," she replied.

"When you say that, is sex considered strenuous?"

"Chase! Doctor, I am so sorry he even asked that." I laughed.

"Oh, Nachelle, do you all really think doctors are so cut dry that we don't know there's only one way babies come along? And to answer your question Chase, you all can still have relations with one another. If there's nothing else, I will see you all back in two weeks."

"Okay, have a good day!" Chase was just the happiest person ever. I guess I was glad because I was sick of his damn attitude.

"Wow, I definitely wasn't expecting that news," I confessed.

"I know, baby. Come on, let's go."

Chase led the way out to the car, and I followed closely behind. This was a bittersweet moment, but it became sweeter once I started thinking about how fun it could be having three babies at once. I also knew it was gon' be a struggle too because newborns needed all the attention you could give.

Chase opened my door for me. We both got in, and he pulled off.

"Chase, Star is upset about something. What did you say to her other than you didn't want another child?"

"I told her I'd never choose her over you, and if you wanted shit with her to end, I'd be down."

"That was so mean. How come when you're with me, you're not like that, and then you talk to Star and you mean as hell?" I wondered.

"She broke my heart Nook, did you forget? This situation is only because of you and for me to see my son more. That's it."

"I understand, but damn, you coulda been a bit nicer about it."

"No, you just hate the fact that I'm blunt, and I don't sugarcoat shit. You know how they say like one woman can change a man, you changed me. You made me see that I could love again and trust another woman, even though you not on board with me about this Bonnie shit."

"Aww, I love you I really do and believe it or not, you changed me too. And it's not that I'm not on board, it's just that the way Diego's wife wants you to go against Bonnie is malicious as fuck. And you don't even know what Bonnie has planned. She could be possibly turning everything over to you once she steps down, and you could just tell Laina to kiss your ass," I mentioned.

"You got a point. I never had that conversation with Bonnie, but maybe I should. And what are we gon' do about Laina if I was to go against her plan?"

"Fuck her. Y'all have killed mafuckas for less, so I'm sure this would be easy."

"Oh, you bold bold, huh? You know that's Diego's wife. We ain't tryna make an even bigger enemy."

Chase made a point. I didn't want anybody coming after us while life was starting to get to where I wanted it to. It was cool, though, because something would have to be done with this bitch period point-blank. I planned to figure something out because Bonnie and Chase are my family, and we all are starting to blend together. The influences of being around them have finally begun rubbing off on me. Nobody will live trying to go against my family.

Chapter 13: Bonnie

Dressed in an Ivory Bell Sleeve Sheath dress by Carolina Herrera, I looked at myself in the mirror and admired how I looked. It traced my curves perfectly, and the sight alone almost made me want to touch my damn self. I smiled as I saw Micah walking up behind me in a black suit jacket made by Burberry with the pants to match. He looked so damn good that I didn't think we were gon' make it to this meeting with Miguel. He got on my nerves, though, because I told him I was going to this meeting alone, and he refuses to let me go by myself.

"The soon-to-be Mrs. Walker," he said as he wrapped his arms around my waist.

"Ooh, I like the sound of that. So, you think you can just smooth talk yo way into going with me?" I chuckled.

"I already told you wassup, don't play with me," Micah responded, laughing.

"You just jealous as hell. Ain't nobody worried about that old ass man." I grabbed my clutch and headed out of the room.

"Yeah aight, if his old ass tries to mack one time and I'mma flat line his ass." Micah opened the front door for me to walk out.

"If he has the balls to do that in front of you, I may have to take him up on his offer because he'd be bold as fuck." I was laughing hysterically, but I straightened that shit up once I saw Micah wasn't smiling, "Damn, I was just playing."

"Yeah, aight," he said before opening my door to his truck, and then he hopped in and sped off.

***

We pulled up in front of Sullivan's Steakhouse and found a park closer to the door. Micah came on my side and opened the door for me. My black Giuseppe heels were all you could hear as we made our way inside of the restaurant.

Stopping at the host podium, I expressed, "Hello, I have a reservation for Bonnie Jones."

"Yes ma'am, it'll be right this way. Follow me." The host grabbed four menus, and my eyebrow rose because it should only be three menus needed.

When we got to our table, I kept my poker face on, but I was irritated because I didn't get the memo that we were having additional guests. When Micah said he was coming with me no ifs, ands, or buts, I immediately informed Miguel of that by text.

"Hello Bonnie, you're looking beautiful as always." Miguel smiled, reaching for my hand to kiss it.

"She's cool, bruh. Who's this?" Micah asked. If looks could kill, Miguel wouldn't even be breathing right now.

"Oh, I'm Rich. I'm surprised Bonnie never talked about me," Rich replied.

"I mean, what would I have to speak about you for? We do business, that's it. I'm assuming that's why you're at this meeting," I fired back. I don't know what the fuck they had planned, but I had enough shit on my plate to have to deal with this.

"Bonnie, it's not like that honestly, why don't you have a seat? We don't want to cause a scene in here," Miguel spoke in a serious manner.

Micah pulled out my chair and then sat down next to me.

"What's this about, Miguel? Because, honestly, I have so much shit going on and people are trying to come against me that I don't know if I can handle y'all being on bullshit too."

"We're here to show you our loyalty. We wanted to personally let you know that no matter what, we're on your side. We both got a visit from Laina Rodriguez offering us your spot. We turned her down. Our belief in your organization is what made that decision for us. You have Rich in Atlanta, me in New York, Chico in Chicago, and soon enough, you'll have someone in Miami as well," Miguel mentioned.

"Who's in Miami?"

"Her name is Mercedes Rosales. Now, I know she's a woman, and you think that nobody could be on your level, but trust me, she's a unique one."

"I'm all for women empowerment — the more women, the better. It's a little too much testosterone around me already. Okay, cool, y'all don't know how much I appreciate you having my back. I don't know what Laina's problem is, but her best bet is to keep my name out her mouth."

I was furious. This bitch had the audacity to try to take shit away from me. Like, bitch you're a woman first. Why would you try to stop the next woman's shine? I was so confused and upset.

"Didn't you say your daddy learned from Diego? Why don't he go and visit Diego to see what's up with his wife?" Micah asked me.

"Good idea bae, that sounds like a plan. I'mma call him as soon as we leave here. The crazy thing is y'all bringing this news to me, and she went to Casino as well, telling him the same thing. According to Nookie, he's really considering it."

"Aww well, ain't no questions as to what needs to happen next, I'll have my shooters come and take care of him," Rich responded.

"Wait, wait, first off we don't need no shooters, I can handle that shit, and secondly, Casino is like my brother, he knows he'd be going against the grain coming at Bonnie," Micah expressed.

"Well, I guess, I'll give you a chance to talk to him, but trust, if he goes on the side of the opposition…"

"Then, his ass is outta here," Micah finished my sentence.

"With that being said, raise ya glasses. We're about to take this shit over, and most appreciation goes to Bonnie for inviting me into this power circle." We all held our glasses up as Rich spoke. I didn't bring up me quitting because my adrenaline was up now, and I was ready to take mafuckas out, then I'd quit.

The rest of the time at the restaurant was a great one. We laughed and threw jokes, ate some good ass steak, and I was about to go home and get some good ass dick.

***

We waved at Miguel and Rich as they each pulled off in their luxurious cars. I looked over at Micah and smiled.

"What?" he asked.

"Don't you feel that rush, the feeling of knowing like there could be a possible war, but you know you on the winning side?"

"I can't deny it. It's definitely a weird feeling. I know one thing, though. I was serious about getting a chance to discuss some shit with Casino. I mean we are practically family, and I was very adamant about not wanting anybody from my family getting hurt again," Micah explained.

"Babe, Casino ain't your family, because if he was, why would he go against the person you love? He wanted to be a part of what I had going on, and now it looks like he was just using the BOTH of us. I'm sorry, I know it hurts, but you have to understand that in this game, it's cutthroat, not love boat." I kissed him softly on his lips and took his hand in mine. Once he understood that I was the only one truly loyal to him, he'd be appreciative.

We walked to the truck hand in hand, and he came on my side to open my door. When I got in the car, my phone buzzed, I looked and saw that it was Nookie calling. I silenced it because I was ready to get prepared for my night with Micah and didn't have time for any negativity with her trying to make me change my mind about Casino. I would just call her back later.

I put my phone up when Micah got in the car because I didn't want to bring that energy back up.

"You gon' call yo daddy to set that up?" Micah was headed towards the highway.

"Thanks for reminding me. I'mma just connect it to the Bluetooth so you can hear too." I called my daddy and connected it to the car.

"Wassup, baby girl?"

"Nothing much, daddy, just left a meeting with Miguel and Rich. I just had a couple of questions to ask you."

"What's going on?"

"Have you heard of a woman named Laina Rodriguez?"

"Yeah, that's Diego's wife. Why you ask that?"

"She's going around to people in MY organization, asking them if they would like to take my place."

"Say what? Nah, Diego wouldn't dare."

"And how do you know it's Diego that's ordering this? She could just be doing it on her own."

"Laina doesn't move unless Diego tells her to. That's how it always been. I'm gonna pay him a visit."

"So, you gon' go to Cuba?"

"Yes, if anybody tries to come against my baby in any type of way, I gotta address it, and it will be in person.

"I'm coming with you."

"No, you're not."

I looked at Micah like he was crazy.

"Aye nigga, you don't tell my daughter where she can and cannot go."

"I do what the fuck I want, nigga. Do you need to be reminded about me, mafucka?

"Chill the fuck out, Micah, damn! Daddy, I'll come over, and we can discuss this then."

"Yeah aight nigga, and Bonnie, I'll see you."

My dad hung up the phone, and I just shook my head.

"The fuck you shaking your head for?" Micah questioned.

"You tripping, forreal, I don't know who you think I am, but this ain't that." I snarled.

"What you mean this ain't that? That's your problem now, Bonnie! You never wanna include me in none of the decisions you make. What the fuck am I even here for?" Micah was yelling at me.

"Micah, what in the fuck is wrong with you, like seriously? If you got cold feet, nigga, let me know now, the fuck? You're not about to keep picking an argument with me every five minutes. You know damn well I'm not the type of bitch you can put in her place!" I yelled back.

"Drive yourself home." He stopped the car on Kessler Boulevard and stared at me.

This was the first time I saw the pain in his eyes. From the moment I first laid eyes on Micah, I could always tell what he was thinking, especially when it came to me. Something was wrong, and I couldn't depict what it was. It was hurting me inside because I didn't want to lose him. He put the car in park and proceeded to get out. By this time, it had started pouring down raining. I jumped out to follow him. I didn't care about this dress or these damn heels.

"Micah, Micah, wait!" I shouted.

He stopped but didn't turn to face me. I met him where he stopped and walked in front of him so that he could look me in the eyes.

"What's going on?"

"I'm not happy with this life no more, and the truth is, you're just getting started. I've been in this shit since I was 13 years old, from killing to selling. I don't wanna do this for the rest of my life. All this damn bloodshed, what's the point of it. Is this really all you see us doing? And then on top of that, I feel like a little bitch that has to bow down to his fiancée."

"I never made you feel that way, Micah! Are you serious right now? And I'm not making you be a part of this, I enjoy doing it with you, but if this is not what you want, then I can't be mad at that."

I was tearing up because it seemed like this was a breakup or something. Usually, I'd be the one storming out and questioning this relationship, but I got past that. I know that I want Micah and only Micah for the rest of my life. The way he talked, it sounds more permanent.

"Bonnie, just give me some time. That's all I need. Every man gets cold feet. I'm sure this is all it is."

"No! I'm not leaving Micah. Now, I'm sick of this. We either gon' get it together, or we not gon' make it. We're not getting into a marriage this way." Tears started mixing in with the rain. I was so tired of all this negativity and drama. I just wanted to live and be happy.

"I gave you your space every single time you disappeared on me, and the moment I need my own, you can't accept it. You're selfish, Bonnie, and the decisions you make shows that. You only care about yourself right now, so when I matter, you call me then and keep the truck." Micah looked me in my eyes, rubbed the side of my face with the back of his hand, and then left me standing there.

"Even when you know all these people are gunning for me, you gon' leave me?" I roared at him.

"See! You're still only worried about you!" I was upset because everything he said was true, and then I just looked like a jackass even more.

I watched Micah vanish down the street before I even moved a muscle. I climbed in the driver seat of his truck and sat there sobbing like a baby. I didn't know where I was about to go, but it damn sure wasn't in the same bed I used to share with him.

Chapter 14: Sniper

"I gotta call Bonnie. I'm sure she gon' be expecting my call," I said to Chandlyn as she laid on her back, inhaling the blunt that I just rolled.

"She gon' be shitty as hell when you don't have good news for her," she responded.

"I know, but you let me worry about that." I pulled out my phone and dialed Bonnie's number. It kept ringing. I was about to hang up until I heard it click over.

"Hello?" she softly whispered.

"What's wrong? You good?"

"Wassup Sniper, it's really not your concern."

"The mission didn't get done."

"What the fuck you mean the mission didn't get done?"

"Look, one of the damn cell mates caught me going in her cell, and I got the dates mixed up with my cousin. He was off that night."

"You real fucking lucky that I have so much shit going on that I didn't call you the night the shit was supposed to happen. Don't think that got you off the hook. The way I'm feeling right now, you bound to take all the aggression I have built up. Get yo shit together!"

The bitch hung up on me after that. My jaw clenched because I was angry as fuck. I threw my phone at the wall, and it fell to pieces.

"What happened?" Chandlyn asked.

"These bitches don't know who the fuck she's talking to like I'm a little bitch or something."

"What you gon' do?" she asked.

"I'mma turn everybody I can against her ass. Make everybody see how sloppy the organization has been in these last few months," I replied.

Sarcastically speaking, Chandlyn asked, "And if that doesn't work?"

See, she was gon' end up being dead forreal if she didn't shut her mouth. I can tell from the short time we've spent together, she rarely thinks of what she says before she says it. Without warning, I backhanded her ass hard as fuck she flipped over from off the bed onto the floor.

"Don't get shit twisted. I can still end you at the drop of a dime. Think about what you say to me before you speak again."

I walked out of the bedroom, leaving her crying on the floor. I wasn't always the type of nigga to lay hands on a woman, but I did when they thought they could speak to me as if I was a female or sum shit. Bonnie would get the same treatment as soon as I could get her alone.

***

I called Casino and asked him if I could meet with him to talk about business, he obliged. He told me to meet him at his crib because he had his son with him. When I arrived, I parked and thought twice about what I was about to do. I knew once I made a move against Bonnie, that the life I had before would forever be altered.

"Fuck it," I said and then hopped out. I knocked on the door twice, and he finally opened the door.

"Wassup, nigga?" We shook up as he let me in.

"Shit nothing much, just spending some time with my son while his step mama and his mama running errands," Casino mentioned while heading to the kitchen, "You can come in here, bro. I don't want us talking in front of my son."

"You make it seem like you know what this is about."

"I know it's about you questioning Bonnie's position, and the reason I know is because I was personally asked to take over."

"By Bonnie?"

"Nah, by her connect's wife."

Laughing hysterically, I quizzed, "And you honestly think that Diego's wife can push Bonnie out?"

"Yeah, laugh it up nigga, but you will be working for me and not Bonnie soon enough."

"Nah, see that's where you're wrong, I don't wanna work for you or Bonnie. I initially came here to see if you wanted to partner up AGAINST Bonnie, but I see you're trying to be in the same spot I'm trying to be in, and that's a problem."

This nigga was delusional if he even thought he'd be chosen before the mafuckas that were working with Bonnie since the beginning.

"So, is that a threat?"

"It ain't a threat nigga. It's a promise. Step on my toes and there will be severe consequences." By this point, we were both itching to pull our guns out our waistbands and get it crackin'.

"Daddy, are you okay?" His son came into the kitchen and asked.

"Yeah, lil man, it's all good, this man here was just leaving."

Casino went and picked his son up and walked to the door. I followed him, but before I walked out, I turned around to make one more point.

"Just to be clear, you're my enemy now, nigga." He slammed the door in my face, and with that, I bounced.

Chapter 15: Reaper

When Bonnie looked me in my face the day she was arrested, I immediately feared for my life after that. I couldn't risk being seen in public. The shit she heard about me on the street was indeed true, but that's because I'm a cop, so of course I'm gonna be talked about. This isn't my first undercover situation, but this was the first time I was afraid. I saw what Bonnie was capable of because she had me participating in some very messed up situations for anybody who went against her.

It didn't hurt that she was sexy as hell, and I even got to taste that sweetness she got in between her legs. Even with that, I still couldn't jeopardize my position. David was really my brother, and she took him away from me. My plan was going perfectly until she gave me the look she gave. My time was limited if these prosecutors didn't get shit rolling quickly. I was supposed to go into witness protection, but they're all filled up. So, right now, I'm just staying MIA.

I was risking it all today, though, because I had to go to the station for a few things I left behind that were important to me. I got out of the car and put my hoodie on nearly blocking out my whole face. When I walked into the station, I showed my badge to the security guard and he nodded his head, buzzing me in. I almost made it to my desk undetected until this jackass pointed me out.

"Well, look who decided to pop in."

I cursed under my breath because this nigga was a crooked ass cop, and I hated him being on this task force. I was shitty that he had to be the one to point me out.

"Lower your fucking voice," I said through clenched teeth.

Roland wasn't shit on a stick, and I could smell him from a mile away. He was sneaky and devious. He worked with the mafuckas we worked hard to put away. I just couldn't prove it.

"I could help you for a small fee. That Bonnie Jones girl, I saw her dude come out the bail bondsman office. I made him an offer for information that could help you." This nigga was thirsty as fuck.

"Nah, I'm good. Besides, you just basically let me know that you work for the bad guys. Meanwhile, I'm putting my life on the line to put them away." I snarled at him. I grabbed what I was looking for out my desk and started walking off.

"You ain't shit but a rat. I want you to remember that you're the lowest of the low," Roland gritted those words through his teeth as he followed me out. This nigga was fucking crazy, and he had me very fucked up. "I'd be careful if I were you, I'd hate for Bonnie to get an anonymous tip."

I turned around to face him quick as fuck and hemmed him up by his collar.

"Mafucka, you wanna try me! If anybody even thinks they gon' come at me, I know who to find first. You got shit confused, and you disgust me. Wait until I tell the captain you've been working with the other side." I pushed him to the ground and looked down at him shaking my head.

"So, you the big bad wolf when it comes to your own kind, but a punk ass bitch when it comes to outsiders." He laughed.

That was it. I was seriously sick of this mufucka. I pulled my Glock out of my waistband and knelt to face him.

"No matter what you say, you can't make me turn into one of them. I'll let shit play out, and I won't be surprised if you get killed fucking with the enemies."

I stood up and put my gun back. After that, I hopped in my car and pulled off.

***

I was beating myself up every single day because even though Bonnie killed my blood, my brother, I still thought about her every day. Shit, it wasn't like my brother was coming back from the dead or anything like that. The hardest part is getting Bonnie to run away with me. I'd be willing to look past her killing my brother if she could look past me getting her arrested. If I go MIA, there's no witness, no trial, and her name is cleared.

I was getting ready to go into the safe house I was staying in until I got a phone call, it was from an unknown number. I usually didn't entertain those, but it could be Bonnie. After dealing with Roland and all his bullshit, I figured he called and let her know something, and she was calling to try to intimidate me.

"Hello?"

"Meet me at Bonnie's old warehouse in Park 100 around 11 p.m. tonight."

"Who's this?"

"Nigga, just be there, and if I were you, I would make sure I showed up."

I knew who it was. This nigga Micah was threatened by me so bad that even when I betrayed Bonnie, he still probably thinks he gotta compete with me. One thing for sure is I was gon' make sure I was there because hopefully, the information I have for him will make him leave Bonnie for good.

Chapter 16: Micah

Leaving Bonnie was very necessary for what I was preparing to do. I was gon' make sure that she didn't have to worry about anything from now on. Sadly, the only way I can even help or interfere with her decisions is behind her back. Once I got back to the house that I had on the market for sale, I went through the last few boxes I had remaining there and put on an all-black Nike jogging suit with some Air Max to match. I grabbed the duffel bag that was already packed up and went to the kitchen. I walked out of the door that led to the garage because there was a Dodge Charger parked there for situations like this. With where I was going, I wouldn't dare want my truck to be in the crossfire. I didn't give a fuck about this car, though. I threw the duffel bag on the passenger seat and pulled off.

I looked at my phone, and Bonnie hadn't called yet. She probably knew that I was right and was really trying to give me my space after all. I was looking at this as a win-win. Maybe it would finally get Bonnie to understand my perspective in this relationship, and then, on the other hand, I was getting ready to get rid of a thorn that was in our side. I almost went through that dumb mafucka who was sitting against my car on the day of Bonnie's bail hearing. I decided against it, though. I was getting ready to meet with this mafucka Reaper myself. If he didn't take the money and walk, I would kill every family member he had left.

***

I arrived at the warehouse and spotted an all-black Honda Accord. This mafucka was being really lowkey. His ass probably was looking over his shoulder every time he moved around. I took it that he was inside because I didn't see anybody standing around. I walked inside the building, and there he was with his hands in his pockets and the hoodie over his head.

"Look, let's cut to the chase. What is this about?" Reaper asked.

"Nigga, you should know. I'll offer you $225,000 to not testify against Bonnie and get ghost," I replied.

Laughing uncontrollably, he stated, "Nah, see, I don't need you to bribe me into running off. I'll do that on my own, BUT, Bonnie will be right with me."

"Nigga, what you say?" My blood started boiling. This nigga was bold as fuck.

"You heard me clearly, nigga. This was all in my plan. I'll get her to turn on you and leave with me."

"You must be smoking dope nigga if you even think she would leave with a rat. You're nothing compared to me. I'm just confused as to why you would even think that she'd do that shit?"

"Oh, you don't know?" Reaper smirked.

"Know what, mafucka?"

I had my hand on my Glock and was getting ready to put one in his dome. See, I was trying to change and not just resort to blowing a nigga head off. After evaluating my and Bonnie's situation, I realized I couldn't keep coming at her about changing unless I'm ready to put my hitman life behind me. My business has grown, and even though I've hired people to take care of my hits, it's still under me. It would all lead back to me, so it was time for me to let it go. Now, Reaper was really pushing my fucking buttons, and I had no problem making him my final victim if he didn't do what the fuck I say.

"I left a lasting impression on Bonnie before all this shit went down, so she'd never want to see me six feet under."

"You right, she won't see you six feet under, but in pieces scattered across the White River."

"Nigga, fuck you. As a matter of fact, I need to thank you. See, if it weren't for you throwing your little bitch fit and leaving when y'all was back in New York, Bonnie wouldn't have been so, hmmm, what's the word? Vulnerable, I guess I should say. My plan came together perfectly."

This nigga was gloating and hinting at the fact that he and Bonnie may have shared something, but I needed this mafucka to spit the shit out, I didn't have time for games.

"And then what? Mafucka, you beating around the bush. You a man nigga, you got two nuts like I do, bitch. Say what the fuck it is you tryna say!" My voice roared inside the empty warehouse. This mafucka was pissing me off.

"You know what I'm saying do the math. You left her, and she came to me and got a real man. I made sure she wasn't missing you, nigga," Reaper gloated.

All I could see was red. Bonnie really fucked this nigga, and we weren't even broken up that damn long. I was about to spazz. Without warning, I took my Glock out and shot him in one of his knee caps.

"FUCKKKKKKK!!!!!!!!!!!!" He knelt to the ground holding his right knee.

"Nah nigga, what the fuck was you saying!"

I marched over to him and started pistol-whipping his ass. He started gasping for air because he was probably choking on his own blood by now.

"Nah, I got a better one for yo ass. We about to take a trip."

***

I threw Reaper ass in the back of my trunk and sped to Bonnie's house. For her sake, she had better be home. If it was any truth to what this mafucka was saying, I was putting a bullet in his dome and calling the wedding off. I don't give a fuck if I left or not, you don't just jump in the bed with another mafucka that quick. For him to be this bulky nigga with a lot of mouth, he could barely put up a fucking fight. Ain't no way another nigga would've hoed me like I just did him. Pistol or not, I just wasn't cut like that.

I pulled up on Hollister, what was supposed to be a 25-minute drive turned into a 15-minute drive. A part of me was livid, but another part of me was hopeful because I knew my bitch wasn't moving that type of way. I didn't even get him out of the trunk right away. I headed straight to Bonnie's front door. I didn't have her key on me, so I just banged on the door until she opened it.

I wasn't surprised when she had a .9mm pointed at my face. It looked like she had just got up.

"So, yo ass was sleep? You really want me to believe that?" I just barged in past her and started looking around.

"Micah, what the fuck are you doing? What's wrong with you??" she questioned.

"WHAT'S WRONG WITH ME? NAH, QUESTION IS WHAT'S WRONG WITH YOU?" I yelled.

"Dude, you are tripping! Nobody is even in here! What the fuck, man?" Bonnie was looking shocked.

"Hold on one damn second," I said and then went back out the front door. I popped the trunk, and this nigga must've been losing too much blood because he was delirious.

"Come on, man, just let me go," he mustered up enough strength to say.

"Shut the fuck up!" I spat.

I dragged Reaper's ass out the trunk, and I was so pissed that I didn't even care that it might be a trail of blood behind me. I threw him over her threshold onto the hardwood floor. All you could hear was his whining while I locked up the house. Nobody was getting out this mafucka until I found out the truth while both were present.

"Micah, what the fuck is this?! You went and found Reaper, somebody who's supposed to be testifying against me at trial! The damn FEDS are gonna be looking for him!!!"

"Fuck that shit! There won't be a trial if this piece of shit is gone! And hold the fuck up is you taking up for this mafucka?" I started walking over to her.

"Micah, no, I'm not. I'm just saying think about this shit for a minute. Yes, I want him dead too, but we were supposed to plan this shit out. Then, you left me in the pouring rain at that. Now, you here talking about getting rid of a mafucka to help me. Yo ass is crazy man, forreal."

I knew the shit seemed weird as hell, but it was all for her good.

"I ain't crazy shit. I had to do it that way because you wouldn't have let me do what I needed to do. So, I did it alone. But, that's beside the fucking point. This mafucka said y'all had relations as in you fucked this nigga. Is that true?"

"W-what?" She stumbled over her words, so I just knew what was about to happen.

"You heard me, Bonnie."

"I don't know what the fuck he's talking about! I ain't fucked him!" she yelled.

"You fucking lying, I can see it in your face! And you don't ever stumble all over your words like you just did!" I got in her face.

"He's lying. I swear, baby, he is! I would never fuck another man after you, I promise." She was crying her ass off by now.

I knelt to face Reaper, and he was looking all fucked up, "So, you lied on your dick nigga? You a real lame for sure."

"F-fuck you. If you gon' kill me, then do it, nigga. Bon-Bonnie tell 'em about how yo taste still lin— "

Blood spat on my face as a bullet went right into the back of his head.

"What the fuck, Bonnie? What did you do that for?" I wondered.

"Fuck him, Micah, damn! The fact that you're sitting there questioning me about anything this mafucka has to say with his rat ass is bogus!" She came over to me. "Micah, I don't give a fuck about no other nigga, and that gesture right there shows that shit. If I wanted somebody else, you know I would've been left by now. You were right, I am selfish, and I do realize that a marriage is a partnership. I can't marry you unless I'm willing to be more considerate, and for you, I will be. You have to give me a chance, Micah, and stop planning severe plans just to prove something."

As she was expressing how she felt, it made me realize how much she was the one for me even more.

"I understand that Chocolate, but you can't just keep making decisions without discussing them with me. Just like now, you killed him, and I wasn't even done gathering all the information I wanted from him. You have to realize that once we're married, I'mma be the one wearing the pants. It should be that way now, but of course, you don't see it that way. I know our relationship ain't gon' be perfect, I know we gon' have our arguments and debates, but at some point, we gotta want this shit to get better."

"It's not that, Micah. It's just that this is all I know, so yeah, it's gon' be a little difficult getting me to be submissive. That's basically what you want me to be. I killed Reaper because I didn't want you to hear that I let him go down on me from him. I wanted to be the one to tell you."

I paused for like four minutes to gather myself, and I sighed heavily. "Bonnie, no more lies. I should not be hearing that from another man. Do you know what that does to my pride?"

"Hopefully, nothing because he doesn't have shit on you and I want you to believe that. You're the only man for me, and I can't wait to marry you. Matter a fact, can't we just skip the whole theatrics and elope?"

"Nope, you're the one who wanted this nice ass wedding, so you gon' get it. We gon' have the best wedding anybody has ever seen in Nap. I wanna show you off to everybody." I grabbed her by the waist and pulled her in for a hug.

"I hope you don't expect nothing with blood all over your face." She chuckled.

"Nah, I'm about to go get in the shower. Call the cleanup crew because there's a mess outside too."

"Wow, you didn't even think about that shit now, did you? I'll just have to see if my guy on payroll at the station will make sure to interfere with the calls that come in about the disturbance. Well, that's if they even saw or heard anything. Shit, we ain't too far off from Moller. They might be used to hearing gunshots." She laughed.

"You crazy as hell. If these white folks see any sight of drama, they're calling the opps. Since you the one that killed him in here, you need to be picking out what carpet we laying down."

I took my shirt off and started heading to the back. I could hear Bonnie making the calls to the crew to tell them to get shit cleaned up in there and outside. I turned her shower on and immediately placed my head under the water. It was so much shit running through my mind. I couldn't help but feel like I lost myself during all that's been going on. I felt like I was always complaining about life, and it wasn't a good feeling at all.

I went back to reminiscing about when I was younger, and my mama was still alive. We always had hard times, but she made sure we were straight and that I still was able to stay in a child's place. I wanted my kids to never even have to think about the thought of struggling.

I felt a pair of hands rub up and down my back, and I closed my eyes because her hands on my body felt good as hell. Bonnie was literally my drug, and I'd go to war with anybody for her. We were toxic to one another, but I didn't give a fuck. This would be who I spent my life with forever. All I wanted to do was eliminate anybody who even thought about going against her or trying to end her life, whether it was behind bars or in the ground. It seemed very contradicting because outside of her, I wanted nothing more to do with this type of lifestyle, but let anybody come at her, and all that shit goes out the window.

Chapter 17: Bonnie

I ran my hands up and down Micah's back. This man was so fine words couldn't even describe him completely. I admitted what happened with Reaper to him because, at that moment, I knew we were gon' be together forever. I used to be the type to believe that marriage shouldn't be thought about at an early age, but when you've met your soul mate, you ultimately know there's no more time for games. It's time to build a legacy. We've been blessed to be in the positions we're in to make enough money to be set for life. Not everybody has that type of lifestyle.

Micah turned around to face me, and I placed my lips on his chest. I began kissing him down his eight-pack, and then I was face-to-face with the monster that knows how to hit all my spots just right. I took his dick into my mouth and ran my tongue around the tip. I could feel his body shiver. I started massaging his balls as his dick went in and out of my throat.

"Fuckkk! You handling that mafucka, huh?" he groaned as he grabbed a handful of my hair.

Micah started fucking my face as tears began flaring up in my eyes. He busted all down my throat, and I swallowed every bit of it up. I didn't let him out my mouth either. I needed to get him right back up so that he could break my back. When he got back hard, he picked me up, and I wrapped my legs around his waist. He slid right inside of me, and I threw my head back into the water and went into pure ecstasy. He put my back against the wall of the shower and hit every spot I had. I could feel my muscles clenching around his dick, and all you could hear was my screams echoing off the shower glass.

"Yesss, Micaahhhhh, oh my godddddddd!" I moaned.

He turned off the water and walked into the bedroom. He laid me on the bed and put my legs up by my ears. My eyes rolled to the back of my head as he dove his tongue deep inside of me. He sucked on my clit as if it was his last meal on earth. I gripped the back of his head, pushing his face deep in my juices. He slid two fingers inside of me while flicking his tongue all around my lips and back to my clit again. I was in heaven. I was almost certain this was what it would be like.

"Babbbyyy, pleeeaseeeee! I'm about to cummmmmmmmm!"

I screamed loudly as I reached my peak. Micah kissed me from my thighs then up my belly. Once he got to my nipples, he took the left one into his mouth and then slid his dick back inside of me. I opened my legs wider, so he could go deeper. I gripped my hands on his ass pushing him inside of me as he sucked on my neck.

Whispering in my ear, Micah emphasized his raw thoughts, "This is my pussy. Don't you ever let another man get close, or both of you will die."

I didn't know why, but that shit made me cum even harder. I was getting ready to become an entirely new Bonnie because from now on, I was submitting to this man. It wasn't even a question about it.

"Flip yo ass over," he ordered. I was so weak because he had made me cum multiple times. I got on my stomach and arched my back. Micah gripped my hair and started smacking my ass as he pounded me from the back.

"Fuckkkk! I swear I'd kill anybody over this pussy. Take all this dick."

He started going faster, and it was to the point I had lost my voice, I knew he was lowkey punishing me for what I did with Reaper. Finally, Micah released himself inside of me and fell on the side of me. I couldn't even say anything. I was asleep within the next second.

***

I woke up the following day very sore from what Micah put on me the night before. I looked around and didn't see him. I immediately got worried because I was out like a damn light. I didn't even wake up or move an inch all night. I jumped up and looked for something to throw on. I grabbed a spaghetti-strapped tank top and some biker shorts. I walked through the house calling his name, but he didn't answer me. My heart was beating fast as hell, I saw that there was no blood in the living room and the blood trail was gone. I smelled food cooking though, so he had to be in there.

When I turned the corner, I saw him in the kitchen cooking. I rolled my eyes because he had me worrying for nothing. He had his AirPods in, so I saw why he couldn't hear me. I tapped him on his shoulder, and he flashed that sexy ass smile at me. He then took one of the AirPods out.

"Good morning sunshine, you hungry?"

"You know I am, baby. You had me worried. I called your name like 1000 times."

"I'm sorry, baby. It's a good day today."

"Why are you so happy?" I quizzed.

"Because we got rid of Reaper's ass, and you know what that means."

"What does it mean, baby?"

"They ain't gon' have no choice but to throw your case out."

Micah was happy as hell. He started making our plates, and I instantly had a flashback to when we had our first rendezvous.

"You're right, but there's still another problem," I mentioned as I grabbed two wine glasses and the orange juice and champagne out the fridge.

"What other problem? Come on now, Bonnie. Don't ruin it for me."

"Baby, I'm not trying to ruin anything, but remember I told you about Chandlyn and that I was gon' have her killed in jail? Well, the dumb mafucka I told to do it didn't do it."

"What the fuck you mean he ain't do it?"

"He didn't do it, talking about his cousin had the date mixed up or some shit, and one of the cellmates across the way was gon' catch him."

I took a bite of the eggs and almost had a food orgasm. Micah had put just the right amount of cheese in the eggs, and he knew I loved cheese so much.

"I see you like them eggs."

"Yes, I love them. You outdid yourself forreal."

"So, what the fuck needs to be done now? And who did you get to do the hit?"

"Sniper's ass."

"Who the hell is Sniper? Where he come from?"

"Man, you asking that should've been the exact reason why I didn't use him. He's one of my runners, but he mostly works out east. You know we don't fuck with the eastside like that, but he brings in a lot of revenue on that side. Easy brought him on when I first started. He just always be thirsty for me to notice him, so I gave him the job since I didn't wanna get my hands dirty and now look."

I was so annoyed with the nigga. I was gon' pop up on his ass. I knew where all my runners stayed so that wouldn't even be an issue. He had just better hope his plan would be in motion or else.

"Well, we have no choice. You know what need to be done. His ass being brought on by Easy should've been a reason not to use him either. And this will be the last time we do some shit like that after he's dealt with."

"Wait, so you wanna kill Sniper now? I don't have any reason to off the nigga right now."

"Why would he fuck up a job like that? How long did it take for him to tell you he couldn't do it?"

My eyes got big because it was a little over a week before the nigga told me about it.

"Okay, just let me find out what I can find out about the shit, and then we can put a plan in motion."

"And what about this trip to Cuba with your pops?"

"Pre-honeymoon vibes?"

"Shit, I'm with it. We can invite Nookie and Casino too."

I rolled my eyes.

"Why you do all that?" he questioned.

"Because this nigga is gon' be on the opposite team, I don't wanna spend my vacation with him, and then I'll have to deal with being around Nookie with a guilty conscience."

"What are you guilty of?"

"I've been neglecting my godmother duties, and then on top of that, I've been taking out my frustration with Casino on her." I was sick thinking about it.

"Just make the shit right, and you can't be a bad godmother when the baby not even here yet. She knows you have a lot going on. Sis will understand, but you gotta open your mouth up for anybody to know how you're feeling." Micah made all the sense in the world.

"I hear you."

"Look, Casino's not about to just say fuck you like that. I'mma find out what the word is for sure, and the perfect time to do so will probably be before this trip. I'mma link up wit 'em."

"What you got planned for the day? Maybe you can throw that in your day, so it'd be handled," I advised him.

"Shit, I was gon' go look for my tux and then meet the cleanup crew at the landfill. I guess I can throw that in there."

"So, you just gotta be with them when they disperse Reaper's body around?" I snickered.

"Hell yeah, I need to make sure that mafucka's never coming back. I wanna make sure that even his spirit be scared to come back."

"Yeah, okay, that mafucka's getting ready to haunt yo ass as we speak." I laughed so hard.

"See you later, Chocolate." He came over to me and kissed me on the lips.

"I love you."

"I love you too, babe."

I'm not sure why that eerie feeling I had wasn't going away, but I would be on Micah's line every hour on the hour to assure nothing happens to him. I heard my phone ringing from the back room, so I ran to answer it before they hung up.

"Who the hell is this?" I said to myself.

"Hello?"

"Hola, Bonnie."

It was a Mexican sounding lady, and I didn't recognize her voice at all.

"Who's this?"

"It's Mercedes. Miguel said that you'd be expecting my call. I guess he left that part out, huh?"

"Girl, you know how men are. He didn't tell me you'd be calling. How are you, though?"

"I'm doing good, getting ready to check on some important information with my man, but I just wanted to check in with you. I'm in your city right now and wanted to know if you wanted to meet me somewhere to discuss terms?

"Yeah that's fine, I was just about to get ready. You can meet me at this venue I was looking at for a business I was thinking about opening, and I can handle two birds with one stone. I'll shoot you the address."

"Aight you got it, mami."

I hung up the phone and proceeded to get ready for the day, I smiled at the thought of me going legit. The idea I had would be major if it all went through smoothly with getting the permits and stuff. Micah was gon' be happy as hell too. It was a dedication to my mama and his as well. I couldn't wait to see the look on his face once it was up and running.

Chapter 18: OG

I couldn't believe where I was right now. This shit was blowing my mind. When I got off the phone with Bonnie the night, she told me about Laina trying to overthrow her, I coughed, and in my hand, there were specks of blood. I didn't know what the fuck that shit meant, but here I was sitting here at the doctor to find out. They had just drawn blood, and I was waiting for the results from that. I looked to the left and smiled when I saw Mercedes walking back in from getting coffee.

"What you smiling so hard for, papi?" she asked me.

"At yo fine ass. You're here with me, and I appreciate that. I know you got more important stuff to get into."

"Stop it. Nothing would be more important to me right now than to make sure you're good. Did the doctor come back in yet?" she inquired.

"No, not at all. This shit is crazy. I'm only 47, and I don't need any bullshit coming my way. I try my best to stay in the damn gym and here comes this shit." I shook my head.

"We gon' be positive, okay? We won't know what's going on until your bloodwork comes back."

"My daughter is gon' blow a damn gasket once she finds out about this shit, and we're supposed to be going out of town for an important mission. I gotta be A1." As soon as I said that, the doctor walked in.

"Okay, Mr. Jones, I read over the results that came from the bloodwork we drew, and there are a couple of alarming factors. But, before I can let you know exactly what it is, we need to conduct an MRI to see if there's a tumor or any other abnormality that would be linked to your kidneys," the doctor relayed.

"My kidneys? Why in the hell would anything be wrong with my kidneys?" I asked more to myself than him.

"Well, there are several things, but it could be something that has to do with older age, smoking, or even high blood pressure. And if you want me to be quite hones— "

"Of course, I want you to be honest, the hell?" He just had struck a nerve. I was so sick of doctors beating around the damn bush.

"Your blood pressure is extremely high. It's to the point where you would be admitted if it doesn't go down by the end of this visit."

"Oh no, I can't stay here, doc. I got shit to do."

"Darryl, listen to him, this is your health we're talking about."

"I understand that, but my daughter needs me. I got shit to handle."

"No, your daughter needs you alive. What would happen if you were to get worse because you decided to put your needs last? I'm sure she rather you take care of yourself first."

Mercedes made a lot of sense. I just didn't understand why I had to be the one going through this shit. My daughter already lost a mother. She didn't need to lose me too. I was gon' do whatever it took to make sure my health was intact, and that started with getting this MRI.

"How soon can you do the MRI?"

"We have about three patients ahead of you."

I couldn't take the chance I needed to know as soon as possible. I pulled some money out of my pocket. It was all one-hundred-dollar bills.

"How much would it take for you to make me first in line? I seriously don't have any time to waste." The doctor's eyes grew wide.

"Sir, put your money away. I'll work something out. I have a daughter too, so I know how it goes."

"I appreciate that so much, doc." We shook hands, and then he stepped out.

"Your daughter must really be somebody special."

"She is. Her mom died when she was 13, and I just want to make sure I'll be the one walking her down the aisle."

"Ooh, so she's getting married soon?" Mercedes smiled.

"Yes, speaking of, would you be my date?"

"You know, I will. Do you and the groom have a good relationship?"

"Nah, not at all. I couldn't care less for him, but he was there for my daughter before I came back. I do want to dead the beef we have for each other to make her happy."

"Well, what's stopping that from happening?"

"Us. We're the ones keeping it from being squashed. We're men, so it's our pride that constantly gets in the way."

"You're her father, and now something could possibly keep you from being a part of their lives. I say you should be the bigger person." Again, Mercedes made a lot of sense, and I took everything she said to heart. I grabbed her hand and kissed the back of it.

"Don't hurt me like the last bitch did. I really like you, and I would hate to have to end you due to the pain you cause me."

"And vice versa. Darryl, you don't scare me, matare por tu polla." When she spoke in Spanish, my dick immediately stood at attention.

"Man, what did you just say, it sounds so sexy."

"I'll tell you later, just know I'm not the one to play with either. I've been dealing with clowns ever since I moved to Miami. Who knew I had to mess with someone from a state I never been to before I met you to find someone solid."

"I'm as solid as it gets. Trust me. There ain't shit but clowns out here. I'm just a rare breed."

"That you are." Mercedes stopped and looked at her phone.

"You gotta go?" I asked.

"Nah, not right now, I'm going to stay here while you get your MRI. Hopefully, your blood pressure goes down so that you can go home tonight. Lord knows I've been wanting to climb on top of you in that hospital bed."

Mercedes bit her lip, and at this point, all bets were off. If I was gon' die, I was gon' die a happy ass man, forreal. I grabbed her by the waist and sucked on her bottom lip. The doctor knew the right time to come in because right before she was about to climb into my lap, the door opened.

"Alright, Mr. Jones, we're ready for you." I got geared up to go take the MRI now.

***

I was thankful after the MRI was done because my blood pressure went down. I just knew being anxious about that damn test was gon' cause my blood pressure to be through the roof. Truthfully, Mercedes calmed me. She was like a breath of fresh air. I knew I shouldn't have been getting too attached because of what just went down with Bebe, but Mercedes was different. She wasn't my age, but she wasn't just a young girl tryna get ahead either. She was 34 years old and on her shit.

I learned a lot about her once we linked up when she landed in Nap. It turns out that she ran the Northeast side of Miami. It's crazy because if I would've known who she was when I was down there, we would've done more than just get rid of Jose's ass. I would've advised her to claim the Southwest side of Miami too. I wasn't worried, though, because I'm sure she and Bonnie would be able to make a deal. I didn't tell her much about what Bonnie did because after the Bebe situation, I didn't want her to think I was just quick to hop into relationships. Then, I would have to hear 'I told you so' repeatedly.

Mercedes and I departed from each other after I was discharged from the ER. She said she'd slide through later.

I parked my car in the driveway, and when I got out, I felt that feeling like I was being watched again. I scanned my neighborhood to see if I saw any unknown cars or anything suspicious. My eyes stopped on a red Nissan Maxima across the street parked on the curb. I just shook my head. This bitch was watching me all this damn time. After she left my house, when I caught her there after that bullshit went down, I never saw her again.

"Fuck this shit. It's about to end today."

I stormed towards her car, and she started it up. She probably was gon' run me over because she thought I was gon' kill her. I stopped in front of the driver's side window and tapped my finger on the glass. She let the window roll down halfway.

"May I help you?" I asked.

"Hey, I just wanted to make sure everything was okay with you." She spoke in a child-like manner.

"Okay with me? Why would that even concern you anymore?"

"Darryl, I'm sorry okay? I want to work things out with us."

Cracking up, I asked, "Have you lost it? You played me to the left, and now you want me to even consider getting back with you? It was never real, remember?" This broad had seriously lost her mind.

"I didn't mean that. Darryl, I have nowhere to go. Star isn't talking to me, and that was like my best friend, I can't go back to Nookie's shop. I was a better person when I was with you." She started shedding some crocodile tears, and I knew even then that she was still full of shit.

"Even if I entertained the thought of us being back together, it'd be long gone because I'm seeing someone else. I don't wanna see yo ass outside of my house again. If you want to keep your life, I suggest you never even come back to this neighborhood." I walked off after that.

She was sick in the head if she thought I'd accept the shit that she put me through. She was behind me now, and I'd be damned if she found out anything about my health. Now, I'mma just go inside and prepare myself for this trip to Cuba in a couple of weeks, I'd worry about the MRI results once we got back.

Chapter 19: Mercedes

I was excited to meet Bonnie at the location she sent to me, which was an empty building that looked like it used to be an old daycare. I pulled up next to a nice ass Porsche. I could see she was doing the damn thing, and I wanted to be a part of her organization. I didn't see her standing outside, so I assumed she was inside. I went through the double glass doors, and it was very spacious. It would take a little remodeling to get it up to par, but it overall looked like a good investment. She was standing there on her phone as I walked up.

"How are you?" I asked.

"I'm fine, and you?"

"I'm great. So, are you looking to buy this place?"

"I've already bought it. I'm thinking of making it an after-care center for the neighborhood kids. I grew up on Kessler Boulevard, so I just wanna bring something productive to it. I'm gonna name it after my and Micah's mom."

I observed Bonnie as she talked about this venture, and she seemed excited about it.

"Wow! That sounds like it'll turn out to be amazing. I'm initially from Sinaloa, Mexico. We don't really have happy endings out there, which is why I'm grateful to have made it out. I reside in Miami now," I explained.

"Yes, Miguel told me you have leeway out there. Do you run the entire city?"

"No, I mostly handle the Northeast side. There was a guy named Jose that used to run the Southwest side, but he's out of the equation now. So, this would be a great time for me to step in and claim it."

"Jose? Why does that name sound familiar, I mean, I know there's a thousand of 'em, but pertaining to this, I think I know who you're talking about." She looked puzzled like she was deep in thought.

"Yeah, girl, I was a part of a whole plan to get rid of that cabron because he was a rat."

"Oh yeah, I definitely know who you're talking about now. He's responsible for Diego being put away."

"It's cool though he'll never tell on another person again. Matter of fact, my guy friend Darryl, came down there from here to get rid of him," I expressed.

"Wait, who?"

"Darryl, girl. He's this fine ass man that I laid up with when he was in Miami, and then we concocted this plan toge— "

"Pauseeee I don't wanna hear nothing else. That's my daddy, Mercedes." She put her hands over her face and just shook her head back and forth.

"Oh shit, are you serious?"

"Girl, yes, you didn't notice that when you first saw me? We're like twins."

"Damn, now that you mention it, you do look just like him. I'm sorry, Bonnie I had no idea. This world is so damn small."

I couldn't believe that I had let the cat out the bag without even knowing it. I hoped that it didn't fuck up any chance I had at making a deal with Bonnie. I needed her product in Miami because once Jose turned up missing, the supply stopped. I was getting my product through Jose because that was the deal we had for me to stay on my side of Miami.

"Mercedes, you seem cool, I really don't have no problem with you dating my father. However, I don't want to mix that with business. He's already overprotective and just imagine how overbearing it'll be knowing his girlfriend AND his daughter are still in this business," she replied.

"I understand that Bonnie, but you're opening up a business now. Clearly, you're trying to go legit, so he probably will just back off."

I thought about how he reacted when we were at the hospital. I didn't think it was my place to tell Bonnie anything about him going to the hospital because I'd be taking that moment away from him.

"You don't know him that well then, him and my fiancé are like raging bulls, especially when it comes to them being coo with each other. Ever since I got shot months ago, they just won't let me make a move without breathing down my back."

Throwing my hands up in the air, I expressed, "Well, shit, that's why Bonnie! You had me thinking they were like that for no reason. You clearly got people gunning for you mami. I'm surprised you don't have any type of security or bodyguards."

"I don't need no damn bodyguards, I already tried that, and he turned out to be a damn snake, an undercover cop at that. Speaking of, how do we know you're not one?" She put her phone down on the podium that was in there and headed towards my way.

"You can check me for a wire or anything you want. Shit, ask your daddy. He knows I'm not a pig." I smirked. She made a look of disgust, and I started cracking up.

"You lucky I'm vibing with you, or else I woulda popped your ass just now for that visual." Bonnie was cracking up.

"Look, you have my word, if you connect me in with you guys and be my supplier, y'all can count on me for anything."

"I appreciate that. I think we could work something out. I want all the women in my life in a position of power. Now, my best friend is not really cut out for this type of business, but she knows now how to stand her ground regardless of what the situation is. She was also shot last year and even attacked while she was pregnant with my god baby. So, we try our best to make sure she's able to protect herself."

"Wow, y'all have been through it this last year, huh? Bonnie, I'm gon' be completely honest with you, and I don't want you to take offense to this at all. What if your fiancé and father are right? Just listen to everything you just told me. Why was your best friend attacked? What is it because they were trying to get to you?"

I honestly was curious because if things like this kept happening, eventually the person or whoever it was wouldn't stop until Bonnie was dead.

Tears started falling down her face, "Do you know how hard it is to maintain a poker face? Or to not be able to open up and vent because you're afraid that person is gon' take the information you gave them and run with it?"

"No, I can't say that I do because I never have to do that," I replied.

"It's not fun. Do you think I don't know that everyone around me is a target because of the position I'm in? If you think that, you're wrong. I never made everybody stay down with me. They have their options."

"Wait, I don't want you to feel like I'm bombarding you or being in your business. I just know that people in a position that we're in, we rarely get to vent or show people how much we're hurting inside. The people the closest to you aren't leaving because they love you and don't want you out of their lives. You have to come to some type of balance, though, that won't put them in harm's way just because they're a part of your life."

"Okay, Iyanla." She laughed. "Nah, but you have some good points and the first step starts here. I got investments into a few restaurants, but this is my vision right here."

"Well, let's get it started then."

"You want to be a partner?"

"Of course, shoot, we can always clean the money through here."

"You right, but I wouldn't be all the way legit if I did that." She laughed and then stopped.

"What's wrong?"

"I think you may be perfect for my daddy. He doesn't have a lot of light around him, and you'd bring him that. I'm such a cold-hearted bitch, and you got me laughing and crying and shit. Y'all will have no problem from me during your relationship. The last girlfriend he did have I didn't approve of. She used to be one of my best friends, and she got with him for payback. She claims my fiancé was her fiancé first. I had no idea they even knew each other. So, yeah, this world is small as hell."

"Bonnie, there is one thing I wanted to mention to you. Just check on your father and make sure he's okay."

"What do you mean?"

"I can't say. It's not really my place, but just make sure you check on him. I'll be heading to him a little later, but I just thought I should mention it to you."

"Okay, thank you. I'll check on him. I just have to handle a couple of things first." She grabbed her phone and then we both headed back to the double doors to walk out.

Once we were outside, we heard some type of altercation a couple of doors down.

"Bitch, where the fuck my money at? You thought you were gon' be able to hide, huh?" The man was choking up a girl that was dark-skinned. She had long, pretty hair. It was unfortunate that she was dealing with a man like that.

"Wait a fucking minute, I know her!" Bonnie said and then started to head over there.

"Wait, Bonnie! Wait!" I shouted after her. I saw her reach into her waistband in the back of her jeans, and out came the .9mm. I'm like oh shit, somebody about to get it.

"Let her go!"

"Bitch, who the fuck are you?" the man asked.

POW!

She shot him in the foot.

"Fuckkkk!!! Bitch I'mma kill you!"

He immediately unhanded the girl, and she looked over at Bonnie in defeat. Bonnie grabbed her by the arm and pulled her to the side, I followed because I didn't want to leave Bonnie by herself, so wherever she moved to, I was moving.

"Who the fuck is that, Star?"

"He's just some little dope boy out of Haughville."

"Haughville? Why the fuck are you dealing with a dope boy in Haughville, ain't you with Casino and Nookie?" Bonnie questioned and then turned to me. "Long story, I'll explain later. Now back to you, what's going on?"

"I'm not about to tell you shit in front of a bitch I don't even know. Why are you even worried about it? You don't like me all because Nookie and I are close," Star said, rolling her neck.

"Girl, calm your ghetto ass down, I don't give a fuck about you and Nookie little fuckship y'all got going on. I was trying to make sure you were cool because I know how much Nookie cares about you. I heard him say you owed him money. You must be on that shit."

"Fuck you, Bonnie. Just telling all my damn business in front of somebody I don't even know." The girl snatched her arm away from Bonnie and went to her car. Once she was in, she sped off.

"That's what I get for trying to help somebody."

"Some people you can't help, and if she's on the powder, it's gon' take more than just you to help her, Bonnie."

"You're right, I'mma have to let Nookie know wassup so they can look into that."

After the commotion settled down, we departed ways. I was feeling very confident about my new partnership with Bonnie. We were about to take over everywhere, and once we started washing money through the businesses, the FEDS would never be able to link anything back to us.

Chapter 20: Casino

I hit up Micah to see if he wanted to go on the basketball court and take it back to the old days. He agreed so that's where we were headed. He came and picked me up, but he ain't know that I invited OG to come out with us. He was just gon' meet us up here at Riverside Park. He parked the truck, and we hopped out. I started dribbling the ball and ran up to the rim, throwing a lay-up.

"That punk ass shot, you gotta slam that mafucka." Micah grabbed the ball and dunked it, hanging off the rim.

Laughing, I responded, "Yeah, aight nigga, you gon' break yo damn back doing that shit. You know I'm too short for all that. I can't do that shit."

"Yeah, I know. Damn it's dead den a mafucka out here. Remember last summer when we all was out here, me, you, Chocolate, and sis?" Micah said, reminiscing and shit.

"Yeah, nigga. What you all having memories and flashbacks and shit for?"

"Cause nigga shit is just so damn different now. It's to the point that you don't even know who the fuck you can trust anymore. Knocking mafuckas off is starting to get easier and easier. I'm about to be a family man, and you over there playing Hugh Hefner and shit." He chuckled.

"You wild, nigga. Not Hugh Hefner old ass though, I'm just living. However, that shit was short-lived, Star done vanished. She hasn't even been back for CJ. I mean it's all good with me, but he asks about her, you know?"

"I'm already knowing. You ain't tried to call her?" he wondered.

"Hell yeah, I have, my son tries all the time, her phone goes to voicemail every time. I'mma do some looking, though, because if she back on that shit, I'm getting CJ for good man, I can't have nobody in and out his life like that. It's unstable."

"You right, bro."

"Now, about that trust shit you were saying. Why were you saying all that?" I questioned.

"Bro, you know why I'm saying it. You thought Bonnie wasn't gon' tell me or something?"

"Nigga, I knew she was gon' tell you. What that mean, though?"

"The fuck you mean what it means? So, you really gon' go against the grain like that? You the mafucka who asked me to connect you with her and then you gon' up and try to take her spot, my nigga? On some sneaky shit?" Micah dropped the ball.

"So, what the fuck you wanna do? Cause mafucka somebody came to ME about how sloppy yo girl been dawg. Just because I heard them out doesn't mean I was going against shit."

"You're one to talk about sloppy when yo impulsive ass stays making dumb ass decisions before even thinking. She still looked out for yo ass, and you're preparing to move against her. How you think I'mma let that fly?"

"You're not." We both turned to the direction of the voice that was walking up. It was OG. I was cursing myself because I planned to have this shit cleared up before OG got here.

"What you mean I'm not, and what the fuck you doing here, damn?" Micah asked.

"This mafucka invited me, but from the conversation I was just hearing, do you plan on making a move against my daughter, Casino?"

"Man, look. Y'all don't even know the whole fucking story, so y'all can chill out with all that bullshit."

"Oh, we don't know? So, how about you enlighten us then?" OG stared a hole through my head.

"Look, the Laina bitch wanted me to meet up with her, I did. She offered me Bonnie's spot. I came home told Nookie wassup, and she immediately called Bonnie. I never even gave Laina ass an answer. Of course, I don't wanna cause no turmoil, but I'm sick of being in the shadows, so I did think about it," I explained.

"See, you mafuckas still too young minded. You worried about being in the shadows when you got more money than these niggas out here, which is all that matters. You can take care of your family. Some of these niggas can't do that," OG commented.

"I understand, but I also have sons to bring into this world along with the one I already have. They're supposed to look up to me, how are they gon' do that in the position I'm in now?"

"Bro, Bonnie and I are about to be out this shit for good! You can have all this shit, my business AND hers, but why would she hand it over knowing you're plotting to get her out sooner than she planned? Just be patient, bro. It'll come. You just have to trust us."

"Y'all don't trust me, but I gotta trust y'all? How that work?"

Micah just threw his hands in the air and grabbed the ball. He started throwing shots. I guess that was his way of blowing off steam.

"Look youngblood, please, don't make me have to get rid of yo ass too. I'm also putting that shit behind me as well. This could be your legacy, and you could be the new boss running this shit. We done did all that we gon' do. I'd rather my daughter have her life while she's still in her prime. I want grandbabies and all that shit. What I'm about to tell you, I don't want his ass or my daughter finding out until I tell them, you feel me?"

"Yeah, I got you, OG."

"I had an MRI done. I've been coughing up blood. I find out the results in about a week or so. If I were to die sooner rather than later, my dying wish would be for you to just let the good come to you. Stop trying to rush it or find different avenues to get to it. And you don't have to worry about Laina either. I'mma handle her ass through her husband. I'm going to see him in person and ask him to look me dead in the eyes and tell me he didn't order anything against my child."

"I hear you OG, and man that's fucked up that you had to have an MRI. I can't believe that shit. I hope it comes through clear, man. And how you gon' see Diego? Ain't he all the way in Cuba?"

"He is, and that's why it's a trip. I can't rely on him giving me the truth through the phone. I ain't worried too much about this MRI. You know me. I'mma keep doing me until the day I die. And if it's coming for me, I'mma go out with a bang."

Micah started walking back up, and we shut the whole convo down about the MRI test, "So?"

"It's all good, bro. Y'all ain't gotta worry about shit from me." I reached my hand out for him to shake up with me. We joined hands and shook up, "I'll tell y'all who you need to be worried about, though."

"Who?" he asked.

"That nigga Sniper, he's a little runner for Bonnie. This mafucka came to my house dawg and told me that I was now an enemy because he planned on going for the same position Laina offered to me. The only thing is he went rogue on his own. I don't know why he decided to go against Bonnie, but she had better watch that nigga. At that moment, I realized we would all be stronger together. So, why y'all coming here making punk ass threats and all trying to punk a nigga, I already made it up in my mind that my loyalty is to Nookie, and she's loyal to y'all."

"Right on, we gon' investigate that shit. Oh, and we ain't gotta worry about Reaper testifying no more." Micah was cheesing hard as fuck.

"Word? Y'all got 'em?" OG asked.

Micah looked at him and mugged him. "Yeah, nigga, we got 'em."

"Bet. Now my baby girl ain't gotta worry about nothing no more. They gon' throw the whole case out. Jose's floating with the fishes down in Miami so."

"Damn y'all the mafuckin' Goodfellas around this mafucka, killing niggas left and right." I laughed.

"We gotta do what we gotta do to protect ours. Micah, why don't we just let this shit go? Let bygones be bygones." OG extended his hand out. Micah took about five minutes before he took OG's hand and shook it while nodding his head.

About damn time, I was sick of these niggas with all that bitch shit. Niggas didn't hold grudges. That's what bitches do.

"Aight then, you mind dropping me back off at the crib, bro? Nookie's been crying about finding Star ass, so I'mma go link with her."

"One," we all said as we went our separate ways. Micah and I bounced, and so did OG.

***

I watched Micah pull off and went into the house. It was quiet as hell in here until I started walking to the back of the house. I heard some sniffing, and I instantly got pissed off. I hated seeing Nookie cry and best believe if it was anything other than mood swings, I was gon' cause hell. I opened the bedroom door and saw her feet dangling off the side of the bed. She was laid on her stomach with her head buried in her hands.

"Bae, you aight? Get off yo stomach. Are the babies coo?" I questioned.

Rising up so that she could be on the side of the bed. "Yes, they are fine. I'm not crying because of them."

"Then, what are you crying about?"

"Star. Bonnie just called me, she saw her over there by One Stop, and some nigga was choking her up about some money she owes him. Chase, do you think she's sniffing that shit still?"

"I don't know, but we definitely can find out. What else did Bonnie say?"

"Shit, that was pretty much it. She said that Star didn't look like herself and that we should see if she's alright."

"Well, we can do that here in a sec. Trust me, baby. She'll be alright. We may have to send her to rehab for a little bit, but she will be fine. I'm not gon' lie, the things I said to her was probably too honest. I'm not saying I led her to do that shit, but it couldn't have helped with the shit I said," I admitted.

I could be the first to say that I was an asshole for the things I said to Star. She was the type of female you couldn't 100% share your true feelings with, or she'd try to jump off the deep end. It was clear that the reason she stayed away was because I told her I couldn't care less whether she was around.

"Damn Chase, you have to find her. I don't care what you have to say to her, just make sure she comes back safely. CJ needs his mother just like he needs you."

"Yeah, but we got you, though."

"And you're right, but we all work better together. It'll be more difficult once the triplets get here." she started, rubbing her belly. I sat next to her on the bed and bent my head down planting several kisses all over her stomach. She started giggling. "That tickles. Stoppp!"

"I got some good news, though."

"Like what?"

"Remember I told you I was playing ball with Micah, I invited OG up there too."

"Oh shit, and how did that turn out?"

"Actually, it turned out pretty damn well. They agreed to let the petty bullshit go, and I decided that I wasn't going against Bonnie after all," I said.

"OMG Chase! Thank God, I didn't wanna have to go through the messiness of choosing you or her. Yessss, this is perfect. Now, we can all really be a big ass family. The babies, then their wedding which, *clears throat*, I'd be waiting for mines shortly, but I ain't rushing nothing." Nookie smiled big as hell, and I could do nothing but smile back.

"Do you know how much I love you?" I asked her.

"Nope, how much?"

"Enough to paint this whole damn city red for you. You are changing me every single day. As much thug as I got in me, you balance me out with your positivity." I grabbed her hands and kissed them.

"You balance me out too, babe. I needed a little roughness in my life. I have to learn how to protect myself. With that shit that happened with Toya, I would never be in that predicament ever again. I got babies to live for."

"The fact that you said that let me know that your loyalty was always with me. There's something I need to tell you, and I hope that you forgive me." I looked into her eyes.

"Oh, hell, no, did you cheat Chase?" Nookie jumped up and got into a fighting stance.

"Man, sit yo big pregnant ass down." I started laughing so hard.

"Nigga, I ain't playing with you, that dick is something serious. I will knock you and the bitch's head off."

"No stop playing forreal. Sit down." I got serious with her. She sat back down.

"I'm the reason Toya is gone."

She got quiet and just stared me down. I couldn't really read her mind or even detect how she was about to respond. Suddenly, she leaned in and kissed me.

"What was that for?" I asked.

"For protecting me, I know why you did it, and I understand. To be honest, it should've happened a long time ago, but I was blind. For that, I'm sorry."

"You have nothing to apologize for. I should've never doubted where your loyalty lies. You're just somebody who loves hard, so when somebody is crossing you, you try to give them the benefit of the doubt. Some people need those type of people in their lives, but not everybody."

"Yeah, I learned that the hard way. I appreciate you, and I can't wait to have your babies. I picked out some names."

While cracking up, I responded, "Oh, Lord, I hope they ain't ghetto."

"Nah baby, for the boys, I chose Cairo and Cash, and for the girl, she's gon' be named with an N like me, Nadia."

"Hmmmm, I actually like those names. That's wild cause I just knew I wasn't gon' fuck with the names you chose."

"Well, I'm glad I proved you wrong. So, since you said you weren't going against Bonnie, does that mean y'all will be planning to make a move against Laina?"

"Yeah, we probably will, but I don't wanna talk about them no more." I started taking my clothes off, and her eyes started getting that seductive look that I loved. "How you want me to treat kitty today?" I softly pushed her down, so that she was lying on her back. I turned her legs to me and started pulling off her booty shorts.

"Whatever you wanna do, baby, you know you please me any and every way," Nookie spoke softly.

"Say less."

I planted kisses up and down her thighs until I reached that spot that tasted just like strawberries. I licked and sucked on her pussy until she creamed all over my face. I turned her on her side and slid in with her right leg hanging across my shoulder. I kissed and sucked on her feet while long stroking her.

"Yessss Chaseeeeeeee, right thereeeeeeee!" she moaned. I palmed one of her breasts and went deeper. Before I knew it, we were releasing at the same time. I spooned her, and we went straight to sleep.

Chapter 21: Laina

"Tek, come into my office, please," I buzzed over the intercom I had installed in my 9,000 square foot mansion. My nephew could be hard-headed at times, but I was ready to put him to the test. I just hoped he'd succeed at what I needed him to do for me. I waited for about five more minutes, and then he came strolling in.

Rushing in, "Sorry, Tia, I was checking in with Siciliy."

"Oh, and how is she? Wasn't she deported?"

"Yeah, unfortunately, she was. We were trying to figure something out before ICE came and got her, but we were too late."

"I'm sorry sobrino. Let me know if you need anything. Well, I may be able to help. I know how much you care for her." I wanted to set this visual up in Tek's mind so that way, he would accept the task I needed him to do if he knew I could help him in this situation.

"How?"

"I have a job that I would like for you to see through and in return, I'd get with my good friend who happens to be a very influential political figure. I know he'd be able to pull some strings in getting her a VISA."

"Wow, Tia, I'd do whatever you want me to do for that to happen. It'd mean so much to me."

"I haven't gotten a call back from Casino. I need you to see where his head is at, and if it's not the decision I want, you take his life. Can you do that?"

"Consider it done. I know just where I can meet up with 'em at too."

"Keep me posted."

I watched Tek as he left out of my office. My left drawer started vibrating, and I rolled my eyes because that only meant one thing, and that was that Diego was calling. I pulled out the burner phone and answered.

"And what did I do to deserve this phone call?"

"Laina, I'm trying to figure out who authorized you to start planning moves against Darryl's daughter?"

"Hello to you too, Diego."

"I don't have time for your bullshit ass games. You're fucking with the business I worked so hard to build up. I just made Darryl the connect over all my distros, and you're trying to replace the distro who's doing the best right now? I don't understand you at all."

"She's getting sloppy, Diego. Too many reports have gone out, the FEDS are sniffing all around, and eventually, she'll fold against all of us."

"That'll never happen. With a father like Darryl, she would never go that route. I never had any issues with her in this business. She's been running her territory for almost four years now. Every now and then, you're bound to have some people trying to come against you and take your spot. It's about how well you conduct yourself that matters. We've all had a bullshit ass arrest because of what the FEDS THINK they know. Yet, we come out on top."

"How can you say that when you're not even here with me right now? You were sloppy too, which landed you right where you are as we speak."

"Who are you speaking to in that tone? Did you forget who I was?"

I took a deep breath and cursed myself. I was afraid of Diego, I honestly was, and I knew he had enough pull to get me handled if I went against anything he said.

"I apologize. Look, I will cool all of this down, and you won't hear anything else about it."

"Good. Oh, and Laina?"

"Yes, Diego?"

"Don't think you know everything, for all you know I could be out sooner than you'd expect."

He hung up, and I looked at the phone as if it was poison. I couldn't believe that he was practically saying he could be getting out soon. I loved him, but I didn't want to be with somebody who I feared. Honestly, I wanted to get rid of Bonnie because she was getting all the praise. Her name spreads around as fast as the coke do. I was envious. Therefore, I was continuing my plan to demote her ass, or maybe I should say eliminate. I would wait for Tek to inform me of how his plan went, and then that will open a whole new can of worms. I didn't care though, the war I wished to create would just be getting started a lot sooner.

Chapter 22: Bonnie

I have to say. It has been a peaceful time over these last couple of weeks. All the bullshit that was popping up seemed to come to a halt. I was grateful because we were getting some lead way for this wedding. I was worried about Nookie because after I told her about Star, we hardly spoke. I don't know if it was just the fact that we all had our lives we were living, or if she was feeling some type of way. I hated the feeling of my friendship slipping away, but I also didn't wanna be the first to reach out either.

I was in my bedroom packing everything up in my suitcase. I was pissed because it looks like I'mma need another duffle bag for this trip. I thought I could fit all my stuff into one suitcase, but it seems like I went overboard. Micah walked in and slapped me on the ass on his way to the closet.

"Babyyyy, I can't fit all my stuff in this suitcase," I whined.

"Shit, I told yo ass we didn't even need that many clothes. Yo ass done turned the trip into a mini getaway." He chuckled.

"That's so not funny. Shit, I figured that was a good idea, that way we can come back and be about all work and no play."

"Yeah aight, you know I'mma always play, especially with that gushy shit you got baby."

"You are such a damn freak. If it were up to you, I would've been had about 40 babies by now."

"Speaking of that, I wonder why you not pregnant yet, I done bust in you so many damn times. You got something you wanna tell me?" He got serious quick.

"No, Micah, I ain't on birth control behind your back, nor am I infertile."

"How you know that? When's the last time you been to the doctor?"

"My annual exam is next month. There, are you happy? You gotta know all my personal business." I smacked my lips.

"Man, if you don't shut that shit up. You know you never told me how you felt about your daddy and me letting the bullshit go."

"That's because you already should know how I feel. I'm happy y'all finally put that shit past y'all, but on the other hand, now I gotta deal with y'all both teaming up against me about getting out the game."

"You ain't gon' have to deal with shit because I'm done preaching about it. You got me sounding like a nagging ass bitch. I'mma just support you until you come to your senses."

"I appreciate that, shawty." I laughed and smacked him on his ass.

"Aye, get off that gay shit." He jumped at me.

"You ain't about that life." I was cracking up, and then my phone rang, "You lucky somebody saved your ass by calling."

"Hey, Nook."

"Hey, chica, are y'all all packed?"

"Girl, I'm still trying. Micah tried to get me to only take one damn bag, but you know how that goes."

"These men don't even know we gotta have a fit for every occasion."

"Period."

"I was just calling because I know we haven't talked much, and everyone has been so busy, but we found out what we're having. We're planning on doing something out there."

"Oh, okay, sounds fun. I can't wait to find out."

"Good. I just wanted to let you know. We'll see you guys at the airport."

"Okay."

I hung up the phone, and Micah looked at me, shaking his head.

"What's that for?"

"Y'all are falling off bad. That was the driest, most boring conversation I've ever heard y'all have."

"I just think we're growing apart. That's it. Ain't nothing wrong with it. We just have our own lives." I finished zipping up my suitcase and set it on the floor.

"Keep telling yourself that Bon-Bon. Just last year, you were about to paint the whole city red because she got shot, and now y'all don't even talk every day. I pay attention to shit shorty. Get that shit together for my nephew."

"I hear you, bae."

"Fuck."

"What?"

"So, I was gon' wait to bring this up when we got to Cuba, but it can't wait."

"Oh Lord, just when I thought shit was going smoothly for us."

"It is, but we have a problem. Remember, I told you to make sure that mafucka Sniper wasn't against you?"

"Yes." I raised my eyebrow.

"I got confirmation from Casino that he's definitely up to some bullshit."

"Micah, what the fuck? When did you find this out?"

"The day yo pops and I let that beef shit go."

"And you just now telling me? Right before we about to be miles and miles away? Who the fuck would even be here to protect my business? This would be the perfect opportunity for Sniper to try to shake shit up."

I plopped on the side of the bed and buried my face in my hands. I couldn't believe Micah right now. Why would he just now tell me about Sniper?

"I'm sorry, damn! Don't you think I got shit running through my damn head just like you do? You should know I didn't purposely not tell you."

"What am I gon' do?"

"Maybe you should invite Sniper to come out there with us, make his ass think that you're testing him for the main spot." He suggested.

"You know what? That's not a bad idea at all. It's brilliant. If he thinks he gon' turn into my enemy, it's best I get rid of him while we're far away. His ass won't even make it back to Nap," I added.

I didn't know why mafuckas steady tried to fuck with me. I didn't like resorting to violence, but it seemed to be the only damn way, and I ain't gon' be the one afraid to get rid of a mafucka who was coming for me.

***

It looked like Micah and I was the first ones to arrive at the private jet my daddy had for us. We were still waiting on Nookie and Casino, and him and Mercedes. He probably didn't think I knew what was going on between them or that I even knew about Mercedes at all, but I couldn't wait to observe how they were with one another. I truly felt like my heart was starting to warm up to people, and the feeling was bittersweet. A year ago, my heart was so cold, and I didn't even entertain the thought of loving somebody after David's no-good ass. This last year alone proved to me that my heart opening had been both a good and bad thing.

Good because I let Micah into my heart, and even though we had our ups and downs, he's been the best thing that has happened to me. Bad, because I'm trusting people too easily, but I feel like it's not my fault, especially when it's some of the people who have been in my life since I started all of this. I pondered on the fact that this aspect of my life may really be over, and I was going to miss it. On the other hand, I was ready to start a different life with Micah and finally be able to live without worrying about something happening to me or the people that I love. Tears began to form in my eyes because I couldn't believe that I wasn't pregnant yet. Micah and I fucked like rabbits, and the fact that I hadn't come up pregnant had me thinking. I told him I wasn't infertile, but who knew?

"Bonnie! Helloooooo." Nookie was waving her hands in front of my face.

"Sorry girl, I had started daydreaming." I opened my arms up to pull her in a hug, "I see that belly is poking girl." We started laughing.

"It is for sure. I'm tired as hell. I just wanna get on a beach and relax. We are gon' have some type of fun on this trip, ain't we?" Nookie flashed all her pearly whites. She was smiling so hard. I couldn't lie. I missed her so much. We used to be together all the time.

"We should be able to do something fun. I was thinking maybe like doing a pre-honeymoon out here too with my baby."

"Yuckkkkk! Girl, I was talking about something for us girls to get into."

"Speaking of that, I'll have to introduce you to Mercedes when my daddy arrives."

"Who the hell is that?" she wondered.

"My daddy's new girl. She coo as hell. You'll love her." I assured her.

I looked around and still didn't see them. I checked my phone because I was waiting on a response from Sniper. After Micah gave me the idea, I instantly text him and invited him on the trip with us. I checked in with him once I got to the jet to make sure he was still down.

"Hell yeah, I'm down but will catch my own flight. I'll let you know when I land."

I slid my phone back in my purse, and we started walking towards the jet. We could at least wait for everyone inside.

"How long have you been Mrs. Friendly, especially with a female trying to be with your dad after what Bebe did?" Nookie questioned in an irritable tone.

"Girl, I've always given people a chance you know that," I replied.

"Yeah, but I'd think since the shit happened with Bebe you wouldn't be so trusting."

"What the fuck is your problem? Like you're the one who kept Bebe around when she should've been cut off a long time ago. You keep throwing Bebe name out and shit. Do you miss her or something? Or is it the fact that I may be developing a friendship with somebody else?"

I was getting very annoyed, and I tried to stay calm because she's pregnant, but she just kept mentioning that bitch.

"I don't have the fucking problem, you do. You can continue to neglect our friendship, but then get geeked about another bitch. Like where the fuck did everything go wrong seriously?"

"Who said anything is even wrong? Nookie, we now have our own lives to worry about. We still check in with one another from time to time. I don't understand what the big deal is."

"How is it not a big deal, and we are both going through major milestones in our lives? I'm about to have kids, and you're about to be a whole wife out here."

"Kids? Did you just say kids?"

"Shit, see, thanks a fucking lot, Bonnie. There goes the surprise." Nookie just rolled her eyes and climbed up the stairs into the jet. Micah and Casino came up behind us with the luggage looking confused.

Rushing after Nookie, I tapped her on her shoulder. "Nookie, you know you heard me, you have more than one baby in there?"

"Try three." She eased her way down into the plush, leather seat.

"Oh my god! Nookieeeeee! I know you happy!" I shouted with excitement.

"I mean, ehhh. It's cool, but you know I'm still being monitored to make sure my placenta stays intact." She rubbed her stomach.

"What you mean ehhhh?" Casino walked through the aisle, asking Nookie.

"Exactly what I said, ehhhh. What if I don't get my body back because of this shit?"

"Girl, you will nowadays girls be popping out babies and don't change a damn lick," I stated.

"And then I be the one to get the stretch marks and shit," she added.

"And? I'd still love you either way, so that's all that matters." Casino came and sat across from me, next to Nookie, and Micah came and sat on the side of me.

"Look, we all are getting ready to come into a whole new realm of happiness. First things first, you two need to hash out every damn thing, and Casino you need to let us know if there's any other bullshit that Laina has planned. Shit's been sweet these last two weeks, but that be when mafuckas try to strike," Micah explained.

"The only thing Laina wants is Bonnie off the throne. She couldn't care less about all the extra shit. I think it's more so jealousy, but yeah, she wants nothing more than to see Bonnie lose it all."

"So, what did she promise you?" I asked.

"All she said was I'd be taking over your position, and when I decline with her, she's gonna just try to get somebody else to come for you. I have no idea what her real motives are."

"Hmmm, what if we let her think you succeeded? She'll put her guard down, and then we can choose that moment to strike against her and get this shit over with. I mean technically, you would succeed, but not the way she wants you to. Y'all about to have three newborn babies, which would make it four children you have to feed. Look, if you promise to take care and protect my best friend and god babies, I have no problem handing it all over to you. I've realized that I had my share of fun in this lifestyle. I'mma continue to have my businesses and investments, but this, I'm done with. Once my name is fully cleared and the rest of my enemies vanish, I will no longer be the queen of this organization."

I couldn't believe I was saying this shit aloud right now, and I didn't feel bad about my decision whatsoever.

"You're my queen and we gon' build a better life for our family and us just watch," Micah chimed in as he pinched my cheek.

"I ain't gon' let you down, Bonnie. I was never gon' go against you. That's why when Nookie called you, I didn't care too much. I did want to be the one to let y'all know myself, but she was being loyal to her friend." He turned to Nookie, and they locked eyes.

"Damn, it's like an episode of *Young and the Restless* on this mafucka," my daddy said as they boarded the jet. We all joined in cracking up. "Everybody, this is Mercedes."

"We've met already," I said.

"Y'all have? When?" He wondered.

"We met up a couple of weeks ago. Miguel told me about the moves she makes in Miami. Casino, I'll let you know everything that I have going on with her."

"Why would he be talking to me about our deal?" Mercedes questioned.

"I'm getting out of the game for good and handing it over to him."

"Oh, okay, I see. Well, it'll be nice doing business with you." She extended her hand to Casino, and he shook it back.

"Aight, let's get out of here." I laid back and prepared to take a quick nap because I wouldn't be getting any sleep once we landed.

***

It was very sunny and warm once we landed on the roof of the Managua Airport in Havana, Cuba. A part of me thought about how Diego was living in prison out here. I doubted that they were nasty and decrepit like Indianapolis prisons.

"Where's the cabana?" I asked my daddy.

"It's about five miles out. Everyone has their own. I'm gonna head out to the prison where Diego is in a sec. Babe, what's the name of the prison?" he asked Mercedes.

"Combinado del Este. It's not too far from here."

"Okay, bet. I wanna get that out the way ASAP so that I can enjoy myself."

"Do you think I should come with you?" I thought it might be a good idea for me to show my face to Diego.

"No, it's gon' be all good. This is lowkey, something between Diego, Laina, and me. It'll be coo before we leave here that's for sure."

We all headed to our cabanas, and while my dad was meeting with Diego, we'd be enjoying ourselves at the beach. Even though I planned on having fun, I knew that one of us was not gon' make it back, and once he landed, he'd regret doing so.

Chapter 23: OG

This prison looked like a damn resort. I should've known Diego would never stay in a dump. It didn't matter if it was a prison or not. I bet he still ran these mafuckas as if he was still on the street. I walked up to the double doors, and they didn't even have metal detectors. There were hardly any guards. I saw the receptionist and stopped there. That way, this process could be a quick and smooth one.

"Hi, how can I assist?"

"You speak English?"

Snickering, she acknowledged, "Yes sir, I speak English."

"I'm looking for a Diego Rodriguez, he's an inmate here, and I would like to visit him."

"Okay, no problem." She grabbed a little microphone looking thing and pressed the button. The music they had playing in the lobby turned off. "Diego Rodriguez, inmate # 85791, has a visitor."

"Y'all real fancy around here. Where I come from, prisons are dumps."

"Oh, we get that all the time. Apparently, the U.S. believes if you're in prison, you should be treated like scum. We don't do that here unless they're rapists or child molesters. Then they don't even make it to a room."

The receptionist started giggling again. I looked bewildered as hell because they were crazy as hell down here.

"Follow me."

I watched her walk around the desk, and she began leading the way. That damn walk was about ten minutes long before we stopped at one of the doors. It just looked like a hotel room door. She swiped her badge, and the door opened.

"Have a nice day." She held her hand out for me to enter.

"You too," I responded, closing the door behind me. "Diego, you got it made in here."

Diego's room or "cell" was decked out with all types of luxurious items in there. He was sitting in a plush recliner that was in the corner. When I walked in, he stood up and greeted me with a brotherly hug.

"Darryl, it's nice to see you. I gotta say I wasn't expecting a visit." He went back to his seat, and I sat across from him on a bench that was against the wall.

"Well, I felt it was necessary, Diego. You know I don't sugarcoat anything, nor do I bullshit around. What is Laina doing making threats towards my daughter?"

"I understand your concern. I can assure you I had no idea that she was even thinking about doing that. I, just like you, was just made aware of this. I still have eyes out in the United States, and it came directly back to me," he explained.

"So, you have some people reporting to you still?" I asked.

"Yes. You see, OG, I'm very comfortable here in Havana because I don't have to deal with looking over my shoulder every five minutes or finding out that someone has decided to plot against me. Even so, I still have to keep my ear to the streets. Laina is only using Bonnie as revenge against me. She's upset that I managed to get myself into what she thinks is life in prison. She doesn't want me out of this type of lifestyle. She's a gold digger and wants nothing more than to live off my income."

"Damn, that's deep. Laina shouldn't go looking for wars that she may not be able to handle. You know I initially thought she was trying to get back at me for what happened all those years ago," I admitted.

"What do you mean? What happened years ago?" Diego questioned.

I started cursing under my breath. This bitch told me she told Diego about it already, and that's why I assumed he knew.

"Wow, so Laina never told you about my encounter with her when I was married to my first wife, Bonnie's mother?"

"Hell no, OG, are you about to sit here and tell me that you slept with my wife?" Diego stood up, and I could see his face turning red.

"Sit down bro." I never even moved a muscle Diego didn't scare me.

"Make some sense of this, please," he said as he eased his way back into the recliner.

"It was the year 2010, and remember, you had just made a deal with them dickheads in New York."

"Right, I remember that."

"She tried to push up on me. I don't know if it was because she was drunk, but my wife wasn't having that shit. I don't know where yo ass was at. You were probably celebrating too much."

"Oh, I do recall something happening between your wife and mine, but it's real vague." Diego looked puzzled.

"Yeah, my wife had spazzed out about it. That shit caused me and her to go at it once we got home because she really thought I had something going on with your wife." I shook my head.

"Them damn women. No, she never even mentioned anything to me about it, so I doubt that would be the underlying reason that she's acting dumb. I will handle it. I just ask that you leave everything alone on your end. I'll make sure Laina is kept in her place," Diego pleaded.

"I hear you, bro, that's why I told my daughter I needed to come look you in the eye because it always answers all of my questions. You can always tell if a man is lying if he can't look you in the eye. You've been straight up with me the entire time. I never questioned you because you always made the right decisions based on instinct. I appreciate you for being my mentor over the years."

I extended my hand to him, and we had a brotherly hug.

"You know we're gon' always be coo and speak facts with one another. We were raised to be bulls in the streets, and I feel like we did a damn good job at running shit. I gotta say, though. You're making me nervous. Why do I feel like this is a goodbye forever moment?"

"It is Diego, it is. Everything I've done did is finally catching up with me. I'm sure I'll have a few enemies in hell if God doesn't forgive me before I die. I've never seen an MRI come back as fast as mine did. I was trying to hold off reading the results until after we left Cuba, but I couldn't help myself. I have stage IV kidney cancer, and eventually, I'll be down because I didn't even know it was this bad. Once you're at stage IV, it's damn near impossible to come out of. I'm not doing any of that chemo shit. Whenever it's my time to go, I'll go. I just hope it's after I walk my daughter down the aisle."

I couldn't believe the words that were coming out of my mouth. I never thought a bitch like cancer would kill me. I thought my death would end with a bullet like I've done to others. This was insane, but I enjoyed the time I did have on this earth. I was gonna make my last few months count and right some of the wrongs that I may have made. Now that everything was good with Diego, and he was going to put his wife in her place, I didn't have to worry about protecting Bonnie because she now had Micah to finish the task. When I'm gone, he'll make sure she's taken care of, especially with Reaper gone, her case is damn near a guaranteed thrown out. I was getting ready to head back to the cabana and enjoy the remainder of the trip.

***

I arrived at the cabana and walked inside the one I shared with Mercedes. When I stepped in, she was bent over putting lotion on her legs, revealing her beautiful set of pussy lips. She probably just got out of the shower. Her body was glistening in the sunlight that came through the blinds. Her hair was flowing down the sides of her arms, and the sight of her just got me on brick right then and there. I walked up behind her and ran my hands up her thighs and then to her breasts circling her nipples.

"Oooh papi, that feels so good," she moaned.

I put my hand in between her legs and started massaging her clit. I slid two fingers inside of her and moved them in and out. She gasped loudly while looking me in my eyes, I placed my mouth on hers, and we shared a sensual kiss. I slid my tongue in and out of her mouth as she matched my pace. I pulled my fingers out of her and slid them into my mouth.

"You taste good as fuck. Lay down. They ain't gon' see us for a while," I smirked.

She laid on her back, and I took off my clothes, leaving just my boxers on. For some reason, she loved it when I kept my boxers on. She was a different type of freak, but I loved that shit. I took her left foot and began placing kisses all over it. I kissed up her leg, and I could feel her body shiver as I got closer and closer to the jackpot. I began feasting on her pussy as if it was my last meal. She gripped my head pushing my face deeper and screaming at the top of her lungs. I flicked my tongue back and forth on her clit as my fingers worked their way to her spot inside of her. I ran my hand over her clit at a fast pace until she squirted everywhere.

"Damn, it looks like you've been dying to get that out, lil mama."

"Lemme ride, papi."

Mercedes got up, and I laid flat on my back. My dick stood at attention, waiting to see her bouncing up and down on it. She took all of me like a pro as she eased her way down on it. She started going up and down as her feet were planted flat on the bed. My eyes rolled at the back of my head because she was gripping the fuck out of my dick.

"Take all this dick," I ordered her. I got her in a bear hug as I plowed my dick in and out of her.

Mercedes began screaming, "Yessss, Darryl, yesss fuck!!!!!!!!!!!!!"

I was pretty sure if Bonnie and Micah were in their cabana that they could hear everything, and I'd be getting cursed out by Bonnie for creeping her out.

I slapped her ass hard enough to leave my handprint. I didn't give a fuck, though, because Mercedes was mine, and it was no going back. I deserved to be with somebody who really gave a fuck and wanted me, not nobody else.

"Shit, shit, raise up. I'm about to cum," I whispered in her ear.

"Cum for me, daddy, cum para mami," she whispered back.

That did it for me. She got me every time Mercedes spoke in Spanish. I released everything inside of her, and she collapsed on top of me.

"For a man that just found devastating news out, you're still able to work that beast you got." She bit her lip.

"I don't give a fuck if I was dying tomorrow. My dick will never stop running." I laughed.

"You so silly. But, I'm so heartbroken right now." She laid on the side of me and started sobbing.

"Cedes, calm down, it's gon' be alright," I consoled her.

"No, it's not Darryl. You're in stage IV, and on top of that, you're declining the treatment."

"Listen to me. I promise to make our last moments the best ones ever. I can't stop what God has planned for me. If it means that I start fighting this shit off, then so be it, but if it means I'll be laid to rest, I'm okay with that too."

I kissed the back of her neck as I spooned her while she cried. I felt tears coming out of my own eyes, but I didn't know what else to do or to say.

"I wish we coulda met a long time ago. I've missed out on so much with you."

"I feel the same way. I love you I really do. I tried my best not to fall for you due to the shit I experienced with my ex, but I'm glad God showed me that I can still love no matter what."

Mercedes turned around to face me and gave me a peck on the lips.

"I love you too, Darryl. When are you gon' tell Bonnie?" she asked.

"I probably won't, not until after the wedding."

"You sure that's a good idea?"

"It has to be Cedes. It just has to be."

Chapter 24: Sniper

Chandlyn and I were in the car on our way to a crucial meet up I had to do before we caught our flight to Cuba. Bonnie had no idea I was bringing anyone, and I planned to keep it that way. I would just drop Chandlyn off at the room before meeting up with Bonnie. I had an ill feeling, though, and I couldn't shake it, so I had something to take care of before I headed out there. I hopped on the I-70 West Highway and headed towards Holt Street, where I was meeting up with someone who would make sure I'd still be able to handle business, whether I was dead or alive.

***

I pulled up to the empty parking lot where City Karz used to be and turned off my lights. I didn't know what time it was in Cuba, but it was getting dark here. It was only six p.m., though.

"Who are we meeting?" Chandlyn asked.

"Just chill out. You don't always have to know every single detail," I informed her.

"Man, if you were gon' bring me around just to mentally and physically abuse me, I could've stayed in jail, or you could've finished the job Bonnie gave you." She smacked her lips.

"That's because I didn't know you were so damn annoying. Like the only reason, I haven't offed you yet is because the pussy and head game's good," I brutally spoke.

"Fuck you, Sniper!" Chandlyn opened the door and started walking off.

I just shook my head. This damn girl was insane like something was off with her. I pulled up alongside her and rolled my window down.

"Get yo ass in the car. I know you cold. It's chilly out here."

"Nah fuck that, I'm sick of you. You're the one who decided to keep me around for your benefit and promised that you'd protect me along the way."

"I am protecting you. No one knows that you're alive. They haven't tried anything with you whatsoever thanks to me." I responded.

"Yet every day I've been with you, you've laid hands on me and talk to me like I'm a dog."

"I lay hands on you in a positive way, so don't even."

"Lies. You smacked the shit out of me just the other day."

"Because you needed it, but don't act like I haven't made your life a little better. Now, come on seriously. I'm taking you to Havana, Cuba. Doesn't that say something?" I smirked.

She just stopped walking and turned to me, then rolled her eyes. I stopped the car so that she could get in, and we went back to the spot where I was initially parked. We were right on time too because the Dodge Magnum turned in and parked on the other side of my car.

"I'll be right back. Here." I gave her a .38 pistol, "Use this mafucka if this nigga gets to being on bs, I'll roll the window down a little."

"Aight."

I stepped out of the car and got into the Magnum's passenger side.

"Wassup, what they call you in the streets again? Sniper?" this clown asked.

"Nigga, you know what the fuck my name is, now look I ain't tryna be here for too much longer. If I don't turn up in Cuba soon, Bonnie gon' be suspicious." I stated.

"You asked to meet me, so what is it that you're needing?"

"I just know a dirty mafucka like you can get this information out about Bonnie if I don't return from Cuba."

"Me? Officer Roland Clark? You think I'm a dirty cop?" He started being sarcastic.

"You are mufucka. Now, can you do this or not?"

"What's in it for me? Money talks, my guy."

"I got 25K in total — 13K now and 12K later."

"Hmmm, I guess that's coo seeing that the lead witness suddenly went MIA, I'm sure they would love new evidence," Roland said.

"Just so you know, I don't want my name connected to this shit at all. I'm not a rat. This recording right here literally has the murder of Reaper on there. They killed him right in Bonnie's living room. You see she didn't know I bugged her place. After she called herself going off on me over the phone, I hatched up a plan to go against her, and when that fell through, this was the only thing left for me to do," I explained.

"Aye, you ain't gotta explain shit to me, but technically if I hand this over to the DA, you, my friend, would be our snitch." He smiled arrogantly and placed his hand on my shoulder.

"Get off me, man, so do we have a deal or not?" I was getting pissed off. This nigga was a certified creep.

"We got a deal. If you don't call me with the rest of the money, then I know you're dead and to release the evidence over." Roland confirmed.

"That's right. Aight let me head on out and catch this flight. Hopefully, I'll be in touch."

"Yeah, hopefully."

I got out the car as Roland thought I didn't hear him say that under his breath. It wasn't as if I didn't have connections my damn self. I'mma look out for me if nobody else does. That ill-feeling, I felt still didn't go away, and I planned to protect myself if it came down to it. All I had to do was play the role of being on Bonnie's side until it was time to come back to Nap, and hopefully, she would believe it.

***

We caught are flight through Delta airlines. Come to find out it was only six and a half hours away. Apparently, Cuba is on the same time zone as us, so we got there around 12:30 a.m. We were staying at a hotel by the name of Meliá Cohiba. I didn't know shit about what was down here, so I chose whichever one looked the best by the pictures. It had beautiful scenery, and I was gon' take full advantage of being here. I planned to enjoy myself because I didn't know if this would be my last chance. Chandlyn went out on the balcony, so I followed behind her. I wrapped my arms around her waist as the wind went through her red hair.

"This is so beautiful. It seems like a good place to escape to. I heard they have hella fun in Havana," Chandlyn mentioned.

"I bet. I just can't see myself living in another country. I'mma just take over Nap, and we'll reign there." I put my nose into her neck, and my dick stood up immediately, "I love that damn cucumber melon lotion you be using."

"You do?" she snickered and started gyrating her ass against my dick.

"You ain't about that life. You tryna throw down right here, right now?" I suggested.

"I'm beyond ready." She lifted her dress, revealing the cash sign she had tattooed on her right ass cheek big ass day.

She had an ass like a peach, and I loved watching that mafucka bounce on my dick. For us to not have known each other for that long, we fucked like there was no tomorrow. I pulled my dick out and ran it up and down her ass. She liked anal, so I knew that was exactly where I was going. I stuffed my dick inside her ass inch by inch, and I could see her holding onto the balcony rails. I spit on my dick and her ass for more lubrication, and that helped a lot. I started fucking her and her screams mixed in with the rest of the town's noises.

"Bend down and grab your ankles," I demanded. She did what she was told, and that allowed me to go deeper. I'm sure she'd be able to feel me in her stomach by now.

We weren't leaving this room at all tonight. I'd leave in the morning. I was ready to finish what we started on this balcony, but all over the hotel room. Tomorrow our plan would begin to be in motion. Chandlyn had a role to play in all this shit too. I wasn't born yesterday. I know Bonnie is upset about me not killing her. She probably has a plan brewing already, but I do too. We discussed it on the plane. All I can say is Bonnie better be prepared for what happens because if not, I'll finally have shit my way.

Chapter 25: Nookie

The next morning after we arrived in Cuba, Chase and I were watching *The Little Rascals*. This was one of our favorite movies. He was massaging my feet as we laid in the bed. I was at the head of the bed, and he was at the bottom.

"Did you call my mama to see if CJ's doing alright?" I asked him.

"Yeah, he coo. Did you still wanna do something for the triplets since that cat is already out of the bag?"

"Nah, I guess we can just celebrate with Bonnie and Micah." I was so down about everything that had been going on. I was excited about having babies, but I was afraid too, and it's like nobody understood that.

"We can celebrate us too. Start thinking about yourself sometimes, baby."

"Yeah, but Chase, do you want me to be honest right now about how I'm feeling about our lives?"

Chase grabbed the remote and paused the movies. "You know I wanna know. I'mma always make sure you're okay."

"I'm scared, Chase I'm terrified actually."

"Of having the babies?"

"Yes, what if something happens during delivery? I'm all the way in Cuba, and my placenta is not even at its strongest. What was I thinking coming here?" I was so frustrated with myself.

"You always second guess yourself. Hospitals are everywhere, babe. I understand you wanna be in Nap but just know if something was to happen, you'd be taken care of. As far as being scared, I know you are. This is your first pregnancy, and it turns out you have to bring three lives into this world. I know you'll be the best thing that has ever happened to them because you're the best thing that's happened to me," Chase vented.

"Aww, I love you. You always know what to say to make me feel better in any situation."

"Love you too. Now, quit all that soft shit, and let's go have some fun or something."

"What do you wanna do?" I inquired.

"Shit, we doing something. We didn't come all the way out here for nothing, so call Bonnie and Micah and see what they on."

"Aight I got you." I pulled out my phone and called Bonnie.

"Nookie, just the person I wanted to talk to."

"That's funny. You see, I was calling you. Wassup?"

"Okay, so, the whole reason for this trip was to get down to the bottom of the bullshit that's been going on with Diego's wife. I also invited Sniper down here because he's apparently an enemy now too. I wanted to see if Casino would be down to help us corner his ass."

"Wow, Bonnie, we were calling y'all to see if y'all wanted to hang out. But, I guess it's all about work down here too."

At this point, I was ready to catch a flight back home. I didn't even listen to what Bonnie had to say. I just gave Chase the phone.

"Wassup?

"We were seeing if you wanted to help us with this situation with Sniper? I mean, you're the one who told us about him plotting."

"I understand that, but my girl wants to spend some quality time and I'mma give her that."

"Okay, tell her she didn't have to get so upset, it's fine. I just wanted to include you, but we'll handle it.

"Aight right on."

Chase hung up the phone and handed it to me.

"Yo ass and all these mood swings. Did you forget we were invited on the trip?" Chase laughed.

"And? Like damn, nobody wanna be doing this shit all the time. I can't wait until she's out of the game."

"Ohhhh now you want her out the game. What happened to girl power?"

"Man, it's still all about that cause she's making her own decision to do so, not because a man said to do it."

"Yeah, okay, I bet if I tell you to do something, you gon' do it." He got up and took his shirt off.

"No, I ain't." I giggled.

"Yeah, okay, Nachelle, keep playing with me."

This man of mine was so damn fine. Everything about him made my body shiver. Chase started tickling me, and I laughed so hard as if I was in middle school again. Then, I felt something coming down my legs.

"I have to go to the bathroom bae," I said. He got off me and went to check his phone.

I waddled to the bathroom, and when I got in there, I could now see what was leaking onto the ground. The red spots of blood were hitting the floor. I felt like time stood still and that I was moving in slow motion. I didn't feel any pain or anything, but at a moment like this, I was supposed to be in Indianapolis.

"Chase!!!!!!!!!!" I screamed. He rushed into the bathroom and looked on the ground.

Frantically speaking, he voiced, "What the fuckkk? Where is it coming from?"

"I don't know, Chase. I guess from my vagina. What if it's the placenta? Maybe I should just call my doctor because it's not a lot of blood and just spots."

"We going back to Nap fuck this shit because if they put you on bed rest, you'll be in Nap. Damn, maybe we shouldn't have come here after all," Chase commented after he went and got my phone. He brought it back to me and then started packing up our stuff.

I dialed the doctor's office, so they could try to connect me with my physician. It was Thursday, so I'm sure she was in.

"Community Network, my name is Rhonda, how can I assist you today?"

"Hi, I need to speak with Dr. Graham, please."

"One moment."

I waited on hold for about four minutes before she came to the line.

"This is Dr. Graham. Is this Nachelle?"

"Yes, Dr. Graham, I'm not in the US right now, and I have a few spots of blood coming out of my vagina. What would you suggest I do?"

"Wait, so you went out of the country, and you're five months pregnant? I understand that you're only in the second trimester, but in your condition, you shouldn't have left."

"I don't really have time for a lecture. I understand that this was a bad decision on my part. What can I do or what should I do?"

"Do you feel any pain in your abdomen at all?"

"No, none whatsoever."

"Okay, great. Get here as soon as possible. Where are you?"

"We're in Cuba."

"Okay, that's not bad. But, we will be closed by the time you get here so I won't be able to see you."

"So, you don't recommend I go to the hospital here?

"Well, Nachelle, you can. I just don't know if they'll have the tools to really help."

"Okay, so in that case, Dr. please, we're willing to pay you whatever you want in cash if you can just make the time to see me. I just wanna make sure the babies are okay."

"Let me know when you all are on the way, we can discuss pricing in person."

"Thank you so much."

I disconnected the call and prepared myself to hop on a flight. Part of me wanted to alert Bonnie, but she had her own thing going on. I just said fuck it, and I and Chase were gone.

***

"You have to call and request a Lyft for us because I don't think we'll have time to go through one of those rental places," I said to Chase as we walked through the terminal.

"Already on it, they should be out there already. You know they be waiting for people to request them. Did you recheck the pad to see if it was any more blood?" he asked.

"Yeah, I checked in the plane before we landed. It should still be okay."

Looking down at his phone, Chase voiced, "Yep, here they come now. They should be right outside the doors."

We walked out of the airport and saw a green Honda Civic waiting for us. I was nervous as hell during the drive to the doctor's office, but I was hopeful. If my babies were okay, I would be perfectly fine with being put on bed rest. Arriving at the destination, Chase pulled out a $20 and gave it to the Lyft driver because he got us here very quickly. We got our stuff out the trunk and walked in. The receptionist was gone for the day. So, I rang the bell and Dr. Graham came from out the back.

"Hey, you guys, follow me."

We left our luggage at the front and followed her to one of the exam rooms in the back. I took my pants and underwear off while the doctor was sanitizing her hands and then putting on gloves. I threw the pad I had on in the garbage and laid on the exam table as she pulled the footrests out, so my feet could be planted flat.

"Alright, open up for me," she ordered.

I spread my legs apart, and she grabbed a towel and started wiping, revealing some excess blood that was there. Chase was hovering over her looking like he was in distress.

"Baby, everything gon' be fine, okay?" I assured him.

"I know boo, I just wanna make sure everything 100 this way."

The doctor slid two of her fingers inside of me. I assumed she was checking my cervix.

Standing up, she removed her gloves and tossed them in the trash, "Nachelle, you got really lucky, your cervix is still intact. I'll grab the ultrasound to do a quick check on the kiddos and your placenta. Blood spotting is not uncommon in any pregnancy, especially with you having triplets. It may be a strain on your placenta, but with good monitoring, everything should be okay."

We both did a sigh of relief as she stepped out to get the ultrasound machine.

"That was close, yeah bae, you just gon' have to be on bedrest til you drop. We can't have these types of problems." Chase approached my side.

"I know Chase, I know."

"You'd probably be able to come out like for Bonnie's wedding since that's coming up soon, but anything after seven months, nope."

"Yes, sir. I know I can never win an argument when it comes to our kids. I can just imagine how it'll be once they're here." I laughed.

"You already know. You might as well prepare yourself to be a housewife or bring the business to the crib."

"I ain't about to be no housewife. That business is mine and will remain mine. I've been doing hair all my life damn near."

"I'm just fuckin' wit you, baby."

Dr. Graham entered the room again with the machine. While she was preparing me to view the babies on the ultrasound, my phone started ringing back-to-back.

"Damn, it's Star."

"You gon' answer it?"

"Hello?" Chase answered, looking pissed off that she was even calling. "Say what? Man, where are you even at?"

I looked confused as hell. I hope Star didn't get herself in trouble.

"Aight man, send me the location. We're leaving the doctor here soon." He was about to hang up, and then I guess she said something else. "Don't worry about why we at the doctor just stay unseen for now."

He hung up the phone and sighed loud as ever. "What the fuck is wrong with her? Like I don't regret my son at all, but she's jumped off the damn deep end."

"What happened?" I asked.

"I'll let you know after we leave." He walked over to hold my hand as we looked on the screen. The doctor used the probe to move the gel all over my belly.

"Woah, we got somebody right here who's camera-ready." Dr. Graham laughed.

"That must be my baby girl." I smiled.

"I'm looking for the other two now. They must be hiding." She moved the probe a little to the left, "Bingo, hey little guy. If you look right there, his legs are wide open showing off his stuff."

"He already knows that's how we do." Chase laughed, and I gave him an evil eye.

"Don't be teaching my son how to hoe around."

"Okay great, I found the other little guy, he's sucking on his thumb. Nachelle, I hate to break the news to you. The babies are fine, but you need to be placed on bed rest for the remainder of the pregnancy. Now, I'm allowing you to do that in the comfort of your own home, but if you get to the point where you go against that and blood pressure and diabetes are brought upon, you'll be a permanent resident in the hospital until you drop," Dr. Graham explained.

"I understand," I replied.

"Great. I'll write up an invoice for you, and then you can wire me the money in the morning, I don't do well with cash." She laughed.

"Thank you so much, Dr." Chase shook her hand and then she left out the room.

"Okay, now what's going on with Star?" I was more worried about that ever since she called.

"She's hiding from some nigga that she owes money to. Bonnie was right. She's on that shit again and must've received some on credit. She knew not to come to me for that shit because I would never give it to her."

"Wow, Star, I just pray that he doesn't find her before we get there."

"Me too, let's go."

***

Chase slowly pulled into an alley in a neighborhood that was downtown off Alabama Street.

"You sure she said she's here?" I questioned.

"Yeah, she dropped the location, and it's coming to here."

He looked around, and we didn't see anybody, or maybe it was too dark. I jumped when I heard tapping on the window glass of the back window. Chase unlocked the doors, and Star quickly got in.

"Go! Chase, go!" Star yelled.

His Challenger sped off in the alley, and we started hearing gunshots. I turned around, and there was a car that was close as hell to ours.

"Get down!" Chase yelled. His windshield shattered, and I immediately got scared for the lives of my babies. I opened the glove department and grabbed Chase's gun. His eyes got wide as fuck.

"What the fuck you think you doing? Get yo ass down," he ordered.

"It ain't for me! You continue to drive, and Star can shoot through the windshield."

"Who is? Bitch you crazy, I ain't getting up off this floor!" Star yelled.

"We're in this shit because of you! Shoot at them to at least get them off our trail! I got babies to live for and not about to get hurt because of your dumb ass choices! NOW TAKE THIS FUCKING GUN, OR IM USING IT ON YOU!!!"

I was irate at this point. She snatched the gun from me and blindly fired two shots out of the broken windshield. They fired two more back. Star finally looked out the windshield and emptied the remainder of the clip. We watched as the car started spiraling and then crashed into someone's garage. We were almost out of the alley when the car blew up and a fire started.

"Chase, get us out of here," I demanded. For the rest of the ride, it was complete silence. I was so fucking upset with Star that I couldn't even think straight.

We got back home, and everyone was still in complete shock. They were in the living room while I was in my bedroom eating some Rocky Road ice cream. I was ignoring her and Chase's ass. I didn't really have a reason to be mad at Chase, but I didn't care. I walked through the living room to put my bowl in the kitchen sink, and that's when somebody finally broke the silence.

"So, you mad at me now?" Chase asked.

"I'm not even mad at you. I'm mad at her ass. I just wasn't ready to go off just yet."

"And what are you mad at me for?" Star questioned.

"Girl, are you serious right now? You jeopardize my life, my babies' lives, today, and then on top of that, I've been blowing you up, and you've been MIA. Then you wanna call a mafucka when you in danger."

"I didn't have nobody else to call! And this is my baby daddy, so of course, I'mma look to him for help."

"I don't fuckin see how! CJ's been wondering where yo ass at and calling you nonstop as well. Any bitch that can go this long without talking to her son is an unfit ass mother," I vented.

"Unfit? I've been doing this shit by my damn self waaayyy before Chase's ass decided to step up. YOU are just mad because I wasn't answering for your own personal reasons. You're not even a mother yet to be sitting here trying to judge me!"

Star was smoking too much of that shit if she thought her not talking to me would be more important than her lack of parenting skills.

"Star, understand this. You were around solely because I wanted you around. I felt like it was a good way to see CJ more, and I could ultimately get the female attention I love. Now, that goes out the window once you start doing basic-bitch ass shit. I'm not even attracted anymore. You tryna come at me about not being a mother yet when I've damn near been a mother to CJ ever since he met me! You can really bounce like forreal!" I pointed to the front door.

"Aye, y'all calm down. All this change and shit just gon' have CJ questioning us even more. Maybe everybody should just have a level head and get some sleep. I would say that Star, you need to detox and go to rehab or something because you not about to have my son around that shit. Like you out here being a powder head. You doing the shit I give to these stings out here. We can't have that," Chase added.

"Y'all don't understand, that's why! I literally feel invisible like I'm a nobody. Chase, you already told me how you felt about me when I asked for a baby. I'm practically nothing to you," Star cried.

"I apologize for the way that I told you how I felt. But, what would you rather have somebody lie to you or be honest?" he asked.

"And even if Chase made you feel that way, I was there for you. I made you feel special, so you can't even use that as an excuse. It's called being strong, and if you feel like you're not getting enough attention, let someone know. But, for right now, you need to get help Star." I walked over to her and held her hand.

"I'll go for my baby because I don't want my son seeing me this way, and I don't wanna lose my life because of this shit," Star admitted.

"What's crazy is you could've easily asked me for the money to pay dude. You'd rather risk your life because of pride?" Chase asked.

"I'm sorry, I really am. Tomorrow I will go ahead and check-in."

"We will be there with you every step of the way. We're family and family disagrees sometimes, but that doesn't mean we don't care about you still."

I hugged Star and started to re-evaluate my life. I think it was time that we left Nap behind. I understand that everybody grows apart, and everybody starts their own lives. However, if the friendship is real, it's supposed to last forever. Not saying there won't be disagreements, but when it comes to a point where you

don't even call to check in anymore, you know it's done. I'd always love Bonnie and appreciate the life she helped provide for my family and me, but it's time we separated our lives from hers.

Chapter 26: Micah

After Casino told us that he was gon' spend some time with Nookie and not be able to help us with this mission, Bonnie and I decided to stake out the hotel that Sniper was staying in. She told me he didn't know that she knew where he was sleeping at.

"How'd you find out where his room was?" I asked her.

"I had to get with my friend from school that works for Delta now. She had one of her flight attendants put it in his luggage. Sniper had better stop playing with me. I'm always two steps ahead. He's up to something."

"I told you his ass was suspicious. I'm glad Casino looked out with the details on what that mafucka was tryna do. So, how you wanna do this? Are we killing him on sight, or do you wanna torture his ass?" I gave her options.

"Nah, I think this is a simple two to the dome type of deal. I was gon' say you can probably go in first and just be hanging like around the lobby and shit, but it looks like they got a restaurant in there, which will be perfect."

"Then, I could order some shit, act like I'm allergic to it and cause a scene. During the commotion, you can just sneak yo way in."

"That's why we're so meant to be. You finish what I'm trying to say." She leaned over and planted a kiss on my lips.

"I'mma fuck you good after this shit. I just know you wanna be the one to get rid of this mafucka. You done had niggas betraying your trust back to back now. It's only right you end their lives since you're the reason they even lived the way they did."

"Exactly, I'm tired of ungrateful ass niggas. It's all good, though. Soon enough, this shit will be over and done with."

I got out of the truck and headed inside the hotel. It was a fancy one, so I knew I had to make this shit believable enough. The host to the restaurant grabbed a menu and motioned for me to follow him.

"Aye, I don't even need a menu, let me get some salmon and asparagus. I don't care how it's prepared just gimme that."

The waiter's eyes just got big as he rushed away. I made sure to sit where I could see everything that was happening from inside the restaurant all the way through the lobby. I checked my phone to see if Bonnie said anything and didn't see a notification. I looked up and did a double take because I saw somebody that I just knew I would never see again.

"I gotta be trippin'," I said to myself. I looked up again and saw that I was not trippin' at all. It was Chandlyn. It all made sense now. Instead of him killing her like Bonnie ordered to do, he kept her alive probably for his own benefit. My plan just went out the damn window. I got up and saw that she was talking to the concierge at the front desk. When their conversation was over, she started heading back to what I assumed was the hotel room. I started walking quickly and was right behind her. I figured they had cameras everywhere, so I didn't wanna pull out my gun. Instead, I grabbed her arm very tight.

"Whoever you are, just know that my boyfriend is upstairs and will kill you," she uttered out.

"Well, that just so happens to be who I'm looking for. Come on. Lead the way," I whispered harshly.

I could feel her shaking because I'm sure she wasn't expecting to see me again in her life.

"M-Micah, what are you even doing here? Let me go," Chandlyn pleaded.

"Did y'all really think he was invited out here on some unity shit? We found out about his little plan to go against Bonnie the moment he said he couldn't finish the job with yo ass. I regret not getting rid of your ass that night." We reached the elevator, and she was hesitating, "Get yo ass on there." I pushed her inside and stepped on.

I pulled my phone out to text Bonnie.

Me: *Plans have changed. Chandlyn is here too. She's taking me up to the room now.*

I was hoping she'd respond quickly, but it didn't look that way. If need be, I'd just have to do the job myself. It was as if we were in slow motion as we waited to reach the 12th floor. We both looked straight ahead, and there was complete silence.

"Where did we go wrong, Micah? Why are we in this place right now?"

She threw out questions back-to-back as if I owed her any explanation.

"The only person to blame for where we are right now is yourself. You decided to make impulsive decisions that cost you your life," I expressed.

"The shit I did was for you! I only left Bonnie's warehouse to come meet you at my house, and then the bitch finds out, and you switched up on me." Her voice started breaking.

"It was the way Bonnie handled herself. It was something I never really seen before. I ain't gotta explain shit to you because we weren't together, so it is what it is. You decided to go against her even after that, so it no longer became a me problem."

My phone buzzed, and I saw it was Bonnie.

Chocolate: *What floor?*

Me: *12th*

"What's the room number?" I asked Chandlyn.

"I'm not comfortable disclosing that." She shrugged her shoulders.

Now, this was the perfect time to pull the Glock out.

"Don't make me ask again."

"Fuck it, Micah! You just gon' have to kill me. This was my last chance at getting a better life, and you and that BITCH are not about to mess it up!" Chandlyn screamed.

I swear steam was coming from my head. She had me fucked up, and at this point, it was only a matter of time before she would be in a permanent nap.

"Don't you think you've already fucked that up on your own? I'm basically giving you a chance, and you wanna hold out for this clown ass nigga. He just gon' kill yo ass as soon as he gets what he wants," I explained.

"What am I supposed to do, Micah? He saved my life in a way. However, I can't deny I still love you. If y'all let me go and I mean forreal this time, like y'all can watch me board a plane tonight for all I care, I will give you the room number."

The elevator doors opened, and Bonnie was standing there looking confused.

"Still playing captain save a hoe, huh?" Bonnie asked me.

"It ain't even like that. I'm tryna get the room number," I said.

Bonnie stepped on the elevator with us and watched the doors closed. She pulled the emergency stop button.

"Ain't none of us leaving out this mafucka until we get the room number, and she's dead."

Chapter 27: Chandlyn

This was it, my last night on earth, I could feel it. My life had been in shambles ever since I graduated from school, and Bonnie was there from time to time when I would fall. However, I grew jealous of her. She would get all the shine while I faded in the shadows. When I met Micah, I just knew he was gon' wife me up, and I was gon' be the arm candy for him, and then guess who came along, Bonnie. I couldn't shake the feeling that I was only alive to be a follower and not my own leader. Micah was right. I couldn't blame anyone for my problems but myself. All the decisions I made may have been peer pressured, but there was no gun to my head for those choices to be acted on.

"Bonnie, what more do you want from me? You sent somebody to end my life in jail, but he didn't do it because some people have a heart. Not everybody always wants to resort to bloodshed," I pleaded.

She started cackling, lowkey making a mockery of me.

"Are you serious right now? Bitch, don't sit there and judge me, talking about Sniper has a heart. Sniper is looking out for SNIPER, you dumb bitch. He could give two fucks about you!"

"Look, we're done playing games. Chandlyn, move your ass right the fuck now and tell us what room he's in."

Micah pushed the emergency stop button back in and the doors reopened. He grabbed my arm, and the tears started flowing down my face. It's cool. I was gon' die sooner or later anyway, whether it was from the hands of them or Sniper's ass.

I stopped in front of door 1203 and pulled out the hotel key card. Bonnie snatched it from me and swiped it on the door. She walked in before me. Once we were all in, I could see that Sniper was in the shower.

"Sit yo ass over there." Micah pointed to the chair in the corner of the room. I sat down and just watched on. When I heard the water in the shower turn off, I braced myself.

"Aye, my little redbone, is that you?" Sniper asked.

Whispering, Bonnie walked over to me. "Bitch, answer him!"

"Yes, babe! It's me."

"Good, I'm about to put it down again on that ass, and then our plan can finally start moving along."

I heard the door open, and Sniper was met with a gun in his face. Sniper didn't even know Bonnie was in the room yet because the way the bathroom was, he'd only be able to see Micah until he turned the corner and that's where Bonnie and I were.

"Surprise, nigga. I wasn't the mafucka you were expecting, was it?" Micah laughed.

"Yeah, aight bitch ass nigga. So, you the mafucka who got Bonnie knocked off her square?" Sniper chuckled.

"The fuck you say, nigga?" Micah popped him in the nose with the gun. Blood flew all over the hotel wall. "Walk over there, mafucka." Micah pointed the gun back at him, and he moved to the of the room where we were. His eyes got big as hell, and as much as he disrespected me, I felt bad.

"Fuck," he mumbled.

"Oh, you thought you were invited here on some kumbaya, shit? Ha, you let your guard down, I see. Don't be mad, though. This bitch done made a few niggas make dumb decisions." Bonnie was throwing a jab at Micah when she said that.

"Man, bitch, fuck you! I know you don't want me to beg for my life cause I ain't that type of nigga. You know what you gon' have to do. Just know I always had a plan to haunt a mafucka once I died."

Sniper gripped the towel that was around his waist. I saw the gun print, and that's when I realized this mafucka must've sensed some shit. I didn't know what to do in this moment, I didn't want there to be a blood bath in here nor did I want to die. I figured I'd save myself and they could just take Sniper's ass and get the fuck on.

"Bonnie, he's got a gun underneath the towel!" I shouted.

"Nigga, what?"

Micah tried to rush over to him and grab the gun, but Sniper's towel dropped, and I almost cried at the thought of not being able to get none from him no more cause I knew he was about to die. Bonnie came and grabbed me by the hair.

"Sniper, I will kill this bitch right here and right now! Drop the fucking gun!" Bonnie yelled as she pointed her gun to my head.

"Man, fuck that bitch!"

Everything was in slow motion at that point. I watched him lift the gun, pointing it at me. Before I could let out a scream, all I could see was darkness.

Chapter 28: Bonnie

Blood splattered all over my face as Sniper blew a hole in Chandlyn's head. I let loose of her hair, and she fell to the floor. Goddamn, this nigga ain't have any sense of loyalty.

"Damn, thanks for handling that for us, but you gotta go too." Micah was standing behind Sniper, and he already had a silencer screwed on his gun, so I just nodded my head for him to do the honors.

Tsk, tsk

Sniper fell face first in the bed, and the white plush comforters started turning bloody red.

"Let's get out of here," I said.

We looked around and realized we didn't touch anything other than our own shit. We put our hoods on and exited the room. These walls must've been soundproof cause the halls were empty as hell. Shit, that was better for us. We made a swift and quiet departure.

***

We were back at the cabana, and honestly, I felt like celebrating.

"We need to call my daddy and Mercedes and see if they wanna go out," I mentioned to Micah.

"I'm good. Don't think I didn't hear that smart ass comment you said in Sniper's room about Chandlyn having niggas making dumb ass decisions," he said while he sat on the edge of the bed cleaning his gun.

"Wow, you really mad about that?" I laughed.

"I ain't mad. You just thought you were slick. That comment had my name all over it."

"Because you could've been killed her ass and didn't. That was dumb."

"Yeah, yeah, shit, I really wanna just head back to the crib."

"To Nap?"

"Yeah."

"Why?" I wondered.

"Because we did what we came here to do. I'm ready to get back to our regularly scheduled program. This wedding is in a month, shit. It's a lot we gotta do. The manager at the barbershop called me before we came out here, and he wanted to meet about a few enhancements at the shop."

"Enhancements? Didn't we just open that damn shop? Everything should be fine."

"I know, but I'mma hear him out. I tell you what. How about we just chill for tonight? Invite them over here, and we'll just drink and play some cards."

"Ooh, that sounds fun. I haven't played cards in forever. My mama used to love playing cards," I said. Micah came and wrapped his arms around me.

"Mine too, baby."

"I gotta surprise for you when we get back home. I don't really wanna tell you until I figure out what the name will be, but you're gonna love it."

***

My daddy and Mercedes came over to our cabana, and we were having a blast. I had NBA blasting from my phone on the Bluetooth speaker they had in there. Mercedes made some Pina Coladas. She said it was a recipe that her mama taught her when she first turned 21. Micah and I were kicking their asses in Spades.

"Y'all asses cheating, Bonnie, I'm the one who taught you how to play." My daddy laughed.

"I already know that's why I'm better than you. I know all ya little tricks."

"When should we be heading back to Indianapolis?" Mercedes asked.

"I say tomorrow, shit. Ain't no other reason for us to stay out here. We can get some good sleep tonight and then just head out in the morning," Micah responded.

"And prepare for the greatest wedding of 2019," I added.

"Baby girl, I'm so proud of you. Who would've thought that 25 years later, you'd grow into a successful, motivated woman? I'm proud to be your father, I really am."

"Thank you, daddy, I really appreciate it. I applaud you for taking the time to teach me everything I know. If it weren't for you, none of this would've been possible. Even with all the heat I've had coming my way, I still had more good things than bad happen to me."

As I was speaking, I could see his eyes start to water, and that was very surprising for me. He rarely showed me that side of him.

"I gotta tell you something." He reached out for my hand.

The mood changed almost instantly, and I had a feeling that the eerie feeling I was having wasn't for Micah at all, but for my father.

"No, what's going on? Please don't tell me no bad news." I could feel my eyes burning from holding back tears.

"Bonnie, I have to let you know. Can you just listen?" he asked.

I didn't say any words, just nodded my head.

"I have stage IV kidney cancer, and no, I'm not doing chemo or anything like that. When it's my time to go, I will go." He held my hand and the tears just started flowing like a faucet. I already lost my mother and now him. Like I didn't understand this shit at all.

"No, no, no! Can't you just do the chemo, daddy? Why would you not want the treatment?" I yelled at him.

"Bonnie! It's my choice! Let me have that, please."

Micah came over to me and placed his hand on my lower back. "Bonnie, right now, it's about him. If he doesn't want the treatment, you can't make him."

I looked into Micah's eyes, and even though he and my daddy had beef, I could see that he would've never wished this at all. I knew he would never have harmed my daddy to the point of no return because he loved me. So, I took in everything he said and looked around the room. Mercedes was bawling her eyes out, and I felt worse. She didn't even get that much time to spend with him. I said nothing else. I just ran out of the cabana and ended up right in front of the beach water.

My feet were deep in the sand, and I couldn't stop crying. It was indeed the most beautiful sight I have ever seen, and I couldn't enjoy it. The stars were shining very bright and all you could hear was the water. I wrapped my arms around myself and just screamed so loud. This was the story of my life, I guess, but, then again, I couldn't really expect such greatness after all the wrong I've done. Even though I was protecting myself, I continued to go against the commandments, and I believed that God was punishing me for it.

I felt a presence walking up, and I didn't even acknowledge them.

"Bonnie Dior, look at me." My daddy demanded.

I turned to him and could barely see from crying so bad. He said nothing. He just reached his arms out for me to hug him. I cried so bad. I felt like I was 13 years old again when my mama died. We fell to our knees in the sand, and he just continued to hold me as we let it all out. I know I was being selfish wanting him to do chemo, so that way he had a chance at fighting this thing. All I could do now was continue to support him the best way I could. One thing for sure, I was gon' pray that he'd make it past my wedding because there's nothing more that I want than him to give me away.

Chapter 29: Star

Today was the day my life would start to change for the better. I was preparing to check into Fairbanks, the addiction treatment center located on the Northside of Indianapolis. On the way here, I reminisced about all the good times I had before I chose to run to drugs. I can honestly say before Chase came back into me and my son's life, everything was good. I'm not blaming him for me turning to drugs, because at the end of the day, I should've been stronger. I looked over at CJ and held his hand. I kissed him on the cheek.

"You know mommy loves you, right?" I asked him.

"Yes, mommy, I love you too." He smiled.

"Now, I want you to be good for your daddy and Nachelle. They'll be with you while I'm getting better. I'm just a little sick with a cold."

"But, mommy, you could take some medicine. Daddy, can she go to CVS?" CJ asked.

Tears started forming in my eyes, "No baby, I need medicine from an actual doctor. You're so smart. I love it. We'll talk every day until I'm better, I promise."

I couldn't take it anymore. I got out of the car and hit the trunk for Chase to open it so that I could get my duffel bag. He got out to help me.

"I don't need your help," I stated.

"Star, stop. Come on. Hug me." He opened his arms to me, and I just stared at him, He grabbed me and wrapped his arms around my waist, "It's gon' be alright you hear me? You come back at 100%, and we gon' be coo. I promise."

Nookie got out, and Chase broke our hug. I turned to her, and she hugged me as well. I started walking towards the entrance and remembered it was something else I needed to tell them.

"Oh yeah, let me know the minute you drop those babies. I need pictures." I grinned.

"I got you, love. Be safe, and we love you," Nookie said.

"I love y'all too." I walked inside and prepared to lead a new life. When I got out, I'd be a better mother, friend, and lover.

Chapter 30: Casino

We had just left from dropping Star off, and I remembered that Tek had hit me up to meet him to play some basketball, but since Nookie and CJ were down about Star leaving, I thought it'd be best to have a family fun day. Nookie couldn't really go out and have some physical fun, so I just planned to grab some movies and a bunch of snacks for us.

"What y'all wanna eat? Pizza or chicken?" I asked them

"Neither," Nookie said.

"What about you, CJ?"

"I want McDonald's!" he shouted cheerfully.

"McDonald's is what you gon' get then. What about you, big mama? Does that sound good to you?" I asked Nookie.

"Yes, I can go for a filet-o-fish sandwich and some fries. Ooh with a tropical berry Sprite and add cheese to my fish sandwich."

"Aight now." I started cracking up, "I ain't even made it to the damn drive-thru yet."

"My bad." She joined in laughing.

After getting something to eat, I went to Redbox and grabbed a couple of movies. I was ready to relax and chill until it was time to meet Tek on the basketball court. It was gon' be dark, so I really didn't understand why he wanted to meet there. Something told me that this wasn't just a general meet up. Laina must've arranged it or something, and if that was the case, I was going into this very much protected.

***

After making sure CJ was sound asleep, I went into the bedroom to check on Nookie. She was laid on her side with her body-sized pillow in between her legs.

"How you doing, big mama?" I sat down next to her feet.

"Where did this big mama name come from, dang?" She yawned.

"Cause you getting chunky, I told you I love it, though."

"You getting ready to go?"

"Yeah, I gotta meet with Tek, Laina's nephew."

"Why would you be meeting with him?"

"Shit, I don't know. I guess Laina's ready for an answer. I haven't told her anything yet. I'm telling you this because if something happens to me, you know where I was. We're meeting at the basketball court at Thatcher Park in about thirty minutes. If I don't call in the next hour to tell you I'm good, call Micah and OG."

"Baby, wait, maybe you shouldn't go."

"I got to. I need to deliver the message whether I have to kill this nigga, or he just goes back and lets her ass know."

"Please be careful. I'm worried sick now."

"Just breathe, okay? I love you." I leaned in and kissed her.

"I love you too."

I had no choice but to leave her. I hoped I didn't have to get into any bullshit tonight.

***

I pulled up to the basketball courts and saw Tek standing in front of his car with a hoodie on. After parking, I grabbed my semi-automatic pistol and tucked it in my waistband. I got out and leaned against my car as well.

"Wassup, bro?" I asked him.

"You know what this about? We need an answer like right now." Tek unfolded his arms.

"Well, you can tell Laina that I said thank you, but no thank you. I'd rather gain the business the most loyal way. And according to OG, her husband demanded that she let this shit go that she has against Bonnie," I mentioned.

"Come on, Casino. You have to take this deal, man. I don't wanna have to end shit like this." Tek was pacing.

"End it like what? Tell me what she has to offer you, and I can possibly match that. You'll have a place on my team, and everything will be coo between us. Matter of fact, how about you make her think that I agreed to work with her and then that's when we'll take care of her. All you have to do is let us know where her main headquarters are."

"Man, she's going to help get my girlfriend back from ICE. She was deported last month."

"Look, let me get some time, I can assure you that I'll work with getting her out of ICE's hands. I know people, is she still in ICE, or they've already deported her?"

"No, she's still in one of the cells."

"I just know that just like me, you got kids to live for, and if you would've tried to come at me tonight, you would've lost your life," I blatantly spoke.

"And you really think you'll be able to get Sicily out?"

"I'm damn sure gonna try," I said.

"Okay, I might be able to get in touch with my uncle, and he may be of assistance with Laina," Tek mentioned.

"How? I know that nigga in an uppity prison, but ain't it still a prison?" I wondered.

"My uncle isn't just at a prison. He just requested to be there. See, she's my aunt by marriage. He's my blood uncle. He really needed the perfect moment to get rid of Laina. I just was trying to look out for myself first, and then I was gon' let him know when there was a good time to strike," Tek explained.

"Well, we all have a common enemy. Let's get rid of her, and then we can move forward." I extended my hand out to him. Tek thought about it long and hard before shaking my hand. I was glad to know that I could persuade him into not making this situation a horrible one.

Now that Bonnie would be putting the organization into my hands, I couldn't afford to be as impulsive as I used to be. Therefore,

I was gon' head back home and lay up with my girl. Nookie didn't know it yet, but I was a little afraid to propose. Shit, I look at Bonnie and Micah, and their relationship scares me. I don't wanna be happy as hell and then as soon as a proposal pops up, all hell breaks loose. I'd be glad when my babies were out of Nookie and healthy. I think that would release a lot of stress that we had right now. It was putting a strain on our relationship, and with Nookie's mood swings, it was hard to do anything without pissing her off. Fuck it. This was the time that I needed to propose. At least we could get engaged, and then once the babies were here, we'd be too busy focusing on them to even plan a wedding. For now, I'd head home and lay up.

***

I woke up in the bed with my arm stretched out, but Nookie wasn't laying on me anymore. She walked in, talking loudly on the phone.

"Mama, yes, I've done all that I can do. I have to be on bed rest if you want your hair done just swing by. Okay, love you too."

She hung up the phone and then crawled back into the bed.

"It's only nine a.m. What are you doing up so early?" I asked her.

"CJ wanted some cereal, and now that I can't really do too much, I'm always up early and shit." She slid the comforter over her body.

"I hear you. So, I know you were happy to see me come home last night."

"Yes, I'm thankful everything was okay."

Bing

"That's yo phone, that mafucka jumping," I said to Nookie.

Grabbing her phone off the nightstand, she announced, "Whatever, oh, it's Bonnie." She took a few seconds to read over what Bonnie sent her, "It's an invitation to be her maid of honor." She threw her phone onto the bed as if it was nothing.

"You not excited? I thought you women be geeked for that type of shit?" I laughed.

"I'm not. I'm ready to have my babies and move far the fuck away, leave my old life behind, and the people in it."

"What you mean leave?"

"Chase, don't you wanna start somewhere fresh? Somewhere new?" she questioned.

"Hell nah, see this is what confuses me with you damn women. You didn't want me to go behind Bonnie back and take over that way. We all agreed that I'd take over the right way, and now you wanna leave all this shit behind?" I hopped out of bed, irritated.

"See, that's the problem right there! You, Bonnie and Micah, discussed that shit without even hearing me out. When it comes to this shit, I'm small to y'all. Just because I don't deal or touch the fucking coke, y'all never include me! That's why I get frustrated so fucking much. If I wanted my best friend out of this shit, what would make you think I wanted my child's father to stay in it!" Nookie yelled and started holding her stomach.

"Calm down. We don't need anything happening. Why the hell you never spoke up about it if you felt that way. I mean you had more than enough time to do so." I sat on the edge of the bed.

"Because I would've never been heard. Y'all still do whatever the fuck y'all gon' do."

"Yeah, okay. If you would've told me you didn't want me in this life, I wouldn't have made a big deal about any of this shit. I would've at least considered it." I shook my head I couldn't believe Nookie right now.

"Well, I'm asking you to let this shit go."

"I'll think about it, Nookie."

I just got up out the bed and prepared for my day. All I've ever wanted was to be the leader of my own organization. The shit was basically getting handed to me on a silver platter and now she comes out the woodworks with all this shit. It was something to think about because I had a life to live for my kids. Nevertheless, that was the very reason I need to stay in this lifestyle so that I can take care of them. I went from having one child to four from one pregnancy. I had a lot to think about, but I damn sure wouldn't be able to think with her down my neck. I was just gon' prepare to find out the additional information for Tek, and then I'd worry about this shit later.

***

I made a phone call to Micah and Bonnie so that we could set up some time to discuss this shit with Laina and Tek. They said they were at the wedding venue to make sure it'll fit enough people for the wedding. When I walked in, the place was big as hell. It was at the Ballare Ballroom Events Center.

"Damn, who the hell are y'all inviting? The whole damn city?" I asked, laughing, "I can damn near hear my echo in this mafucka."

"Whatever nigga." Micah dapped me up, and Bonnie waved to speak.

"So, it's almost time, huh? Y'all got about two weeks left and y'all tying the knot."

"Yes, I'm stressed out, I'll be glad when it's all done." Bonnie smiled.

"Well, look. We almost got this other shit over and done with. Laina sent Tek to kill me last night, but she wasn't successful, see I promised him the same thing she did, and that's to get his girlfriend out of ICE," I explained.

"And how the hell you gon' do that? What connections do we have with that?" Bonnie questioned.

"Well, I was hoping that dude that gave you his card Micah, that crooked cop, maybe he knows something," I suggested.

"That's police, though, not deportation, nigga."

"I was just saying he could steer us in the right direction, or shit Bonnie, maybe even your lawyer."

"Man, that nigga is on the straight and narrow, I doubt that he will help us break somebody out of ICE."

"It can't hurt to try, I wanna keep my word with Tek about this shit, I'm tryna start on a good note with mafuckas."

"Okay, I got you. I'll check-in and see what I can find out. Micah, you wanna meet up with Roland or me?" I asked.

"I'll meet with him."

Bonnie's phone started ringing.

"Hello, Diego? Are you out?"

Micah and I were looking on wondering how she was talking to him, but then again, I forgot Tek told me he could do whatever he wants.

"Shit, hell yeah! Thank you so much for including me."

Bonnie hung up the phone and was cheesing hard as fuck.

"What you smiling so hard for?" Micah's jealousy was showing.

"Diego gotta plan to make Laina bow down. He wants me there. Y'all just need to make sure y'all get that set up for Tek."

"And when is that happening?" I asked.

"Tonight."

Chapter 31: Laina

I was pacing my office back and forth. I couldn't believe Tek wasn't answering my calls. All that did was make me worry, and I hated worrying. My door began to open, and I looked confused because I didn't ask anybody to come into my office.

"Excuse me? Did you ask to come in?" I said as the person was walking in. Once the person turned to me, I saw that they had a black mask on, "Who the fuck are you?" I pressed my intercom button to scream help, but it was silent. I got irate because this all seemed like some type of setup.

"You may wanna come with me, and if not willingly, I have no problem forcing you."

"Who are you?" I asked again.

"So, I see you wanna do this the hard way."

The person pulled out something weird and brought it to his mouth. Suddenly, I felt a sting right in my neck. It was a damn spit dart. He had something in there that was making me lose consciousness.

"Somebody h-helppp meeee," was all I could say before I could only see pitch black.

***

My eyes started fluttering, and everything was blurry. I tried to make out the scene of where I was at. I could see a couple of bodies standing in front of me but couldn't make out who they were.

A bucket of cold water was splashed into my face, and that made everything clearer, but it was cold as hell. I could feel that my hands were tied behind my back so that I couldn't wipe my face. Somebody rubbed a towel over my eyes, and then my vision was clear as day.

"Diego? Mi amor is that you?" I questioned.

"Cut the bullshit, Laina. You were going to deliberately go against my wishes and continue to go after Darryl's daughter?" he quizzed.

"I-I was only trying to pr-protect us. She was eventually going to flip on all of us," I stuttered over my words.

"Who was gon' flip?" I heard a woman's voice coming from behind me.

"No, Diego, I know you did not set me up! I am your wife!" I shouted.

"But, you're also causing a lot of friction mi amor, and it actually wasn't me who turned against you at first." He nodded his head over to the left of me. I looked over and in walked Tek.

"How could you?" I asked him.

"I got somebody else to help with Sicily, and they've already sent over proof that they could get her out. You were too messy for business, and on top of that, my loyalty is to Diego, not you."

Bonnie and Tek walked and stood next to each side of Diego.

"Now, why in the world would you decide to come against little old me? What did you gain from that?" Bonnie questioned.

I wouldn't dare give this bitch the satisfaction of seeing me sweat. I wouldn't address her ass either. If she wanted any answers, she'd have to meet me in hell to get them.

"Oh, now you don't have anything to say?" she asked.

"Enough," Diego said. Everybody got quiet as a mouse, "Laina, remember when I said I wanted to leave this life behind, and you made a big fuss about it. That was only because you wanted to lead it, now wasn't it?"

I remained silent, and that pissed him off.

"Everyone, leave now!" he bellowed.

Everybody started exiting, and once the door closed, he slapped the spit out of my mouth.

"You're an embarrassment. Do you know that? You're doing things you have no business doing, running trap houses out of Greenwood, ordering hits, and you had the audacity to lie to me over the phone and think you weren't gonna get reprimanded for that? You didn't want me anymore because I was turning legit all for you to try to run this business?"

I remained silent even after he slapped the hell out of me. Instead of answering his questions, I hawked up more than enough spit to cover his entire face, but I wasn't going to do that. I decided to spit on his feet. He found that very disrespectful, which was why I chose to do it.

"You're gonna regret that. Oh, and you neglected to tell me about all those years ago how you tried to sleep with Darryl."

My eyes got big because I never thought that the secret would get out. I rolled my eyes and started accepting the fact that I just may die today.

"Instead of ridiculing me, why don't you just do what you have to do, Diego? I don't want to be with someone I'm afraid of. Darryl is such a fine man. He moves with finesse, and he knows how to cater to his woman. I was always so jealous of Malorie. She had Darryl wrapped around her finger, and that's why he couldn't see that I would've been a great catch. On top of that, you're trying to go legit, and in so many words, I'm just not attracted to you anymore."

Every word I spoke, I knew I was hitting his pride. This was my first chance to scan the area, and I realized we were in someone's office, but it wasn't his because he didn't have a home located in Indianapolis. I realized we were in my home in Greenwood, and I was gon' die right in my own damn office. I thought they had taken me away.

Diego walked over to me and stared into my eyes. A single tear fell out of his left eye. Suddenly, he wrapped his hands around my throat, and his facial expression never changed and neither did mine. I knew he was hurt by what I said, and I didn't give one fuck. He should've been a better husband to me. He should've continued to provide me with the lavish lifestyle he turned me on to. Now, he was upset because I didn't want this life to slip away from me, so he feels like he needed to strip it away from me. One thing for sure, two things for certain, Diego will die in hell. Just because you wanna turn legit doesn't mean that you'll be forgiven for the many lives you've taken, the dirty deeds you've done, and the lives you've ruined due to performing those deeds.

I know this won't be the last time I see Bonnie, Diego, or even my nephew who turned against me. I felt my life slipping away from me, my blood vessels popping in my eyes, and I watched Diego's mouth curl up into a smile.

I was able to muster out two simple words, "Fuck you." Before I took my last breath and everything went dark.

Chapter 32: Bonnie

Now that Laina was gone, it was official, all my enemies were now gone, and I couldn't have been any happier. After Diego informed us that Laina would no longer be a problem, he announced that he will be returning to Cuba and is out of this life for good. We discussed the fact that my daddy has cancer, and he told me he already knew. He looked heartbroken as well. My father was loyal to many people, and it showed. They respected him, and it was because he was a man of his word. Today we were doing the wedding rehearsal, and I was so excited. We both decided it'd be best to just have Nookie as my maid of honor and Casino as Micah's best man. My daddy was gon' walk me down the aisle, and we'd have a seat reserved for both of our mothers in recognition to them.

It was now six-thirty p.m., and we were waiting for Nookie and Casino to arrive. I understood that she was on bed rest, but the rehearsal starts at seven p.m. I called her phone, and it went straight to voicemail.

"Do you wanna go ahead and start?" Pastor Ramsey asked.

"No, just a few more moments, please. I'll pay you for the additional time. I'm sorry." I looked at him with a defeated look on my face.

"It's fine. I brought my tablet, so I'll work on some things until you all are ready."

"Thank you, Pastor," I said.

"Something ain't right. You and Nookie have had your issues, but it ain't in sis' heart to not be here," Micah mentioned.

"I don't know, Micah. It's been bad, really bad. Maybe this is payback. You already told me how selfish I was, and it probably showed in my friendship too." I admitted.

"Aye, don't even beat yourself up like that. The biggest thing is admitting your mistakes, and you're not 100% wrong in this situation. Both of y'all are. She has something exciting going on just like you do, so she can't be upset that y'all ain't talked that much."

"I still could've been more interactive, but at this point, I just don't know what to do anymore."

"You'll figure it out. You always do." He kissed my forehead, and then his phone rang, "It's Casino."

"Wassup bro, where y'all at? What? You forreal? Aight bet here we come."

Micah hung up the phone and was smiling big as fuck.

"What's going on?" I asked.

"Nookie about to have the babies. He said they at the crib they can't even make it to no hospital. He's scared as hell. Let's go."

Out of all damn days, my god babies had to come today. It was okay, though, because I was just happy that Nookie wouldn't have to continue to be miserable through her pregnancy. We can always reschedule the wedding rehearsal.

After telling and paying the pastor, DJ, and wedding planner for their time unused, we rushed over to Nookie and Casino's place. When we arrived, the door was partially cracked. There was a blood trail possibly leading to where Nookie was, and then we were met with her screams. We followed it all the way to their bedroom and then their bathroom. Nookie was sprawled on the floor with her legs propped open while Casino was against the wall on the floor, holding his head.

"Casino! Seriously! You supposed to be helping!" I yelled and dropped down to the floor to help Nookie.

"Shit, sis, I thought this was gon' be more joyous than this." Micah went over to Casino, "Bro, come on. Snap out of it," Micah said.

"The fucking head is right there. I touched my baby's head! I don't know what the fuck else to do. She's trying her best to keep em in there, but they about to come out!" Casino shouted.

"Did y'all call the ambulance? She not gon' make it to no damn hospital."

"We didn't have time to do that, call 'em for me, bro," Casino said to Micah. I focused my attention on Nookie. She looked like she was in so much pain.

"Nookie, why are they coming three months early?" I questioned.

Sobbing, she cried, "I don't know. My insides hurt so bad. It's like they're trying to slide out, I'm not having contractions, so my placenta must've burst. Get them here now!"

My eyes grew wide as I saw the head sliding out. I grabbed the towels hanging off the rack and put it under her ass.

"Just push Nook, push. We can't reverse it now. One or all of these babies are coming out as we speak," I sternly spoke to her.

"O-okay. Aaarghhhhhhhhhhhhh! I can't hold the baby in any longer." She exhaled, and the baby slid right out. It was so much blood that I was praying that Nookie didn't lose consciousness.

"Casino, come get the baby! It's one of the boys! Bring some scissors for the umbilical cord! He is so small. Man, they needed more time."

I was glad that the baby was out, but still nervous because she had two more to go. It hurt my heart because they were going to be premature. The baby started crying, and my heart began to melt. Casino walked in and knelt beside me. I gave him the baby, and he snipped the cord. Watching him wrap the baby in the towel made me cry.

"Nookie, how you doing?" I asked her.

"The ambulance is on the way. They should be here in a couple of minutes." Micah came back in and said, "Bonnie, why isn't she moving?"

"What you mean?" I looked down at Nookie and saw that she had passed out. "Oh my god! They need to hurry the fuck up! She done lost too much blood, and it's still two babies in there! They're not getting enough oxygen!" I started bawling and panicking. My chest was tightening up, and I just knew I was having a panic attack. Micah came and grabbed my face.

"Calm down, count to ten. Nookie needs you right now."

With each word he said, I just closed my eyes and counted to ten. My breathing got better, and that's when the paramedics came in. I sighed in relief that she could finally get some professional assistance. There were two paramedics, and they got on each side of her. Casino got up and got out the way.

"Sir, she was pregnant with triplets. She still has two left to deliver. Her placenta must've broken, and that's why she's lost so much blood. You have to get her to the hospital ASAP!" I stated.

"Ma'am, let us do our jobs. We'll take care of her," one paramedic said.

"Well, you're not moving fucking fast enough! Y'all can do that BP shit when you get there or on the damn way!" Casino yelled.

The baby started crying again.

"Casino, calm down, you're scaring the baby. Can y'all just please get her to the hospital? We'll follow close behind," I added.

The paramedic looked at me and had sincerity in his eyes.

"Let's get her on the gurney," he said to the other paramedic.

Micah and I hurried to the car, ready to follow them to the hospital. I looked like I had just come out of a murder scene. I watched as they brought Nookie out while Casino followed behind holding the baby close to him. They put Nookie on the ambulance and Casino hopped in with her.

***

I swear it seemed like we got to the hospital in only five minutes. They were speeding their asses off. Micah didn't give a fuck either he just rode with his hazards on to let people know he was following the ambulance. Now I was pacing back and forth, waiting for them to come out of surgery. Casino couldn't go back into the OR with Nookie and the other two babies, so he went to the NICU with the first baby.

I was a nervous wreck. If I lost my best friend before I made things right between us, I would be mortified. I'd give all of this up just to go back to how we were before all of this happened. Who would've thought the most joyous thing could turn into a nightmare in a matter of seconds?

Casino walked out, and I just rushed over to him and hugged him. He and I were never close, but he's been there for Nookie, especially since we haven't been as close as we used to be. While I was hugging him, he just broke down and cried.

"Is everything okay with the babies?" I asked.

"Yeah, they're perfect, I'm just worried about Nook, that's all. I'm sorry," he replied.

"No, you're okay." I waved Micah to come over. He took my place and gave Casino a brotherly hug.

"She gon' pull through, man, I know she is. Sis ain't about to go out like that. She survived the storm, and she'll survive this too."

"Right on, man." Casino wiped his face. The doctor came out and headed over to us.

"Hey, Chase, how you holding up?" the doctor asked.

"I'll be fine, doc, if you tell me my baby's mother lived."

"Are you the family as well?" She looked to Micah and me.

"Yes," we said in unison.

"I can truly tell you that she is one hell of a fighter. She lost a tremendous amount of blood. It looks like her placenta abrupted. Those babies are strong too. They held on and put up a tough fight as well. Of course, you know they were already sent to the NICU. Nookie needs a lot of rest to restore herself. She will need as much help as she can get. We ended up having to do an emergency C-section because she was not conscious to push the remaining babies out. With them being preemies, they will have to be in here for quite some time. Due to the amount of blood loss, and the time she was unconscious, we also had to perform an emergent hysterectomy," she explained.

"Poor Nookie, I thank God she's alive, but how would she feel when she finds out she'll never give birth again?" I looked up and said.

"Thank you so much, all that matters is that they are alive. We'll do whatever we can." Casino shook the doctor's hand. "When can we see her?"

"She's in recovery so you'd have to wait until she's in her room, the anesthesia is wearing off. The babies, on the other hand, follow me." She smiled.

We followed her to the NICU, and we stood outside the door as she took Casino inside. They were all in separate incubators and my eyes began watering. They were gonna have the strength of their mother. She has been through hell and back, and I honestly felt like it was a sign for us to make sure we were back on track. Those babies needed as many people they could to be there for them and I planned to be there every step of the way.

Chapter 33: Nookie

All I could feel right now was pain. My eyes were fluttering and burning due to the light as I slowly opened them. I looked around and saw that I was in a hospital bed. I saw the IV coming out of my hand, which caused me to feel down my stomach. It was very tender and flat, which meant my babies were out, but where were they. I started panicking and trying to find the nurse call light. If this is what after birth felt like, I promise I will never have another child ever again. I pressed the call light, and tears started flaring in my eyes. All I could remember was blood everywhere. I remembered pushing out my first son, and then everything just went dark. Bonnie was so brave with helping me even though she had experienced nothing like it before. I'd forever be grateful to her for that. The nurses came in and were smiling big as day. I didn't understand what they could be so joyful about.

"Hello Nachelle, you're finally up. I'm Nurse Jessica, and this is Nurse Rebecca, we will be your nurses until the next morning."

"Where are my babies?" I jumped straight to it. I couldn't care less about me right now. I just needed to know they were okay.

"They are in the NICU, they were born three months early, so they require some additional help in order to gain the proper weight to be released," Nurse Rebecca stated.

"To be released? What do you mean to be released? So, my babies have to stay in here until when? What are their weights now?" I questioned.

"They are all a little over three pounds, let me grab the clipboard. Cairo is and Cash were both three pounds and six ounces. Nadia weighed four pounds." Jessica stated.

"Oh my god, my poor babies," I cried.

Nurse Rebecca came over to my side.

"I know this is hard for any mother to hear, that her three newborn babies have to be hospital bound until they are healthy enough to leave, but what I can tell you is that they are doing amazing. We've been getting updates from the nurses, and I don't think they'll have any issues progressing."

"Thank you so much. I knew I wasn't gon' be able to hold them for the remainder of my pregnancy. I just thought I'd be more prepared. All I can remember is pushing my first child out, and then everything went dark."

I grabbed the tissue that was on the stand and blew my nose.

"Well, we're here to inform you of all that occurred. You did end up having to have an emergent C-Section. Therefore, you have a bikini cut incision. You'll have to be in here for three days, and then you can be released if you don't hemorrhage or have a severe infection," Nurse Rebecca explained.

"Wow, so I have stitches?"

"Yes, and they will dissolve, so you don't have to worry about that. There is something else we need to discuss with you." Nurse Jessica said, and both she and Nurse Rebecca came back to the sides of my bed.

"What is it? I thought the babies were fine."

"They are. This is about future babies, Dr. Graham had to perform an immediate hysterectomy. You won't be able to have any more children," Nurse Rebecca said in a sweet tone.

"That's it?" I asked.

"Yes."

"Oh shoot, y'all had me scared. I'm happy. After this, I don't want any more kids and then I ain't gon' have to worry about periods no more either. Oh, hell yeah," I responded.

Their eyes were big as ever. I'm sure they weren't expecting this response. I started laughing and then stopped because that just caused more pain. "Where are the pain meds? I know y'all probably think I'm crazy, but this journey has been horrible."

"We just never see such a joyous response for that type of news. It's usually straight to tears," Nurse Jessica commented.

"I understand, but this is probably for the best. Now, where are those meds?"

***

After another thirty minutes, I was finally being transported to my room for the next three days. I still felt some severe pain in my lower abdomen, but I just thought it was a part of the recovery. I'd make sure to address it, though. Hopefully, I can be at peace, and I'd be there for sure once I was finally able to see my babies and touch their little hands. I couldn't wait to see Casino, Bonnie, and Micah. I know they were all worried sick. I hope Bonnie would be able to forgive me because her rehearsal was last night. I didn't expect this to happen, and it just seemed like nothing was in favor of us trying to repair our broken friendship. We arrived at the room and they explained the process for visitors and ordering food from the café.

"Okay, Nachelle, is there anything else I can do for you today? Your family is still in the waiting room."

"There's one thing that I need if you can ask Dr. Graham to come and check on something for me. I understand that I'll have pain because I just was in surgery hours ago, but this is like nonstop it feels like a hammer is hitting something inside of me."

"Oh, wow, let me come check your vitals." She walked over and scanned the screen, "Your oxygen and blood pressure are pretty stable. Usually, if something is alarming, your blood pressure would increase."

"I just don't understand why the pain is this intensified if I'm on strong meds. I don't believe this is normal," I admitted.

"Well, no disrespect, ma'am, but this is your first pregnancy, so you're going to experience some weirdness and, unfortunately, some pain. You went through a lot with doing a partial delivery from the vagina and then the remainder was completed by C-Section. So, it takes a toll on your body," Nurse Jessica explained.

"I understand, if you could have Dr. Graham step in whenever she can, that'd be great. Oh and tell my family they can come in." I was done talking to this nurse. I hated nurses who act as if you should take their word as bond. You're not the doctor, so I want the doctor's expertise.

"Okay great, I'll alert them right away," Nurse Jessica said and then stepped out of the room.

I was pondering on what name I was gon' give my firstborn. All we knew was that he was the boy, but I couldn't look to see if he had something that stood out. I'd decide to name him Cairo once I figured out which one it was.

I started dosing off, waiting for them to come up to the room. That anesthesia was no joke. I heard the door begin to open and woke right back up and in walked Chase.

"Hey, baby." I smiled.

He didn't say a word. He just grabbed a chair and came over to my side. After he sat down, he just started crying uncontrollably.

"Chase, baby, what's wrong? I'm okay." I grabbed the back of his neck and began massaging it.

"You don't know how scared I was, Nook. Everything could've been taken away from me, you and the kids. I didn't know what to do. All I feel like is that I wasn't strong enough for y'all." He grabbed my hand and started kissing it.

"Chase, do you really think I'd hold that against you? Baby, we're still young and never even been through something like this before. I mean, I don't know how Star's delivery went, but I'm sure it was nothing compared to what looked like a massacre in our bathroom. I know you were scared, and I'm just thankful that you and Bonnie made sure Cairo was safe."

"Cairo." He smiled. "He's the firstborn. That name is perfect for him."

"I know. I'm ready to see them," I said sternly.

"I know, boo. Let me go get Bonnie and Micah, though that way we can all head up there together."

"Okay and check and see if Dr. Graham is out of surgery. I need to speak to her about what I'm feeling."

"And what's that?" He doubled back and came by my side.

"I don't know, babe, but it's pure pain. I can barely move, but I wanna see my babies."

"Man, don't make me go curse these mafuckas out," he said.

"No, baby, it's fine. Just ask them if she's out then come back."

He left out, and then Bonnie came in smiling with Micah right behind her.

"I'm so happy you're okay, Nook."

"Thank you so much for helping with Cairo. I don't know if he would've made it out without your help." I reached out for her hand.

"No, thank you for being strong and delivering my god babies. Nookie, I'm so sorry for everything that's been transpiring with us. You know you balance me out. I can be so cold-hearted at times, and you still accept me for who I am. I've been a bad friend, and I just want you to know that I plan on making everything right."

Bonnie started shedding tears, and so did I. We've been through so much together, and it's been hard adapting to the changes we've both endured.

"Bonnie, you know I'll always be there and vice versa. This will be a new beginning for all of us. Girl, you coulda went and got cleaned up. I can't believe you're standing here with all my blood on you." I smiled.

"Girl, that doesn't mean a damn thing. I had to make sure you were straight." Bonnie stepped to the side so Micah could greet me.

"You one hell of a fighter, sis," Micah added.

"I'm just glad we made it out, I'm in a lot of pain, but for them, it's worth it."

"Aight, enough of all this sentimental, we've been big ass babies today. It's time to go check up on the real babies." Chase laughed as he walked back in. "Babe, they said Dr. Graham's still in surgery, so we can go see them, and then she should be done when we get back." I nodded my head in agreeance.

He grabbed the wheelchair and pulled it to the right side of my bed. It was difficult getting out, but I knew I needed this movement. Eventually, I'll start feeling back to normal. After making sure I was settled along with the IV, we all headed over to the NICU. I was so anxious my heart was beating fast.

Once we made it over, the nurse informed us that only two of us could go back at a time.

"Go ahead, y'all. We'll be right out here," Bonnie said.

Chase and I headed inside as the nurse decided to escort us to our babies. My heart broke once we arrived in front of their incubators. They were so small, and all these tubes were hooked up to them. I was so afraid for my babies.

"Aww, my poor babies." I cried.

Chase held my hand as I shed tears for my babies. This was all my fault. Dealing with a psychotic ass bitch caused me to get attacked by her, and now my babies were suffering because of that decision. Their little stomachs were going up and down, up and down. It just seemed like it was so hard to breathe.

"I don't want them seeing my babies like this Chase. This is so hard to deal with."

"I know, baby, I know. They're going to love them, Nookie, you don't have to worry about being embarrassed. They are inspiring."

I slowly stood up, and Chase helped me by holding my arm. I walked over to the first one, and it was my baby girl.

"Hi, Nadia. Mommy's little girl. You're so beautiful," I said to the incubator and then moved down to the right of her, and there was the second baby boy.

It wasn't the firstborn. I could feel that it wasn't.

"Hi, Cash, my baby." His eyes were wide open, and they were the most beautiful set of eyes I had ever seen.

Lastly, I made my way over to the last incubator.

"Mommy's firstborn Cairo, you're gonna be the leader of the pack. I can already tell. I can't wait to y'all get out of here. I have so many plans for us."

"They gon' be the shit, all three of them. CJ is gon' be happy as hell when they come home."

"Yes, I cannot wait until they all can be together. He gon' be a good big brother. I wonder when they can start getting taken out of these things," I said.

"I already asked. They'd rather them be a little bigger, but you can definitely hold their hands now," Chase replied.

"They're so fragile. I'll just wait. What is that? So, they're being fed through these tubes."

"Yeah, Nook, they going through it, but daddy's babies gon' thug it out. I ain't even worried."

"I wish I had your faith. I'm so scared, baby."

"I know."

"I just wanna be with them all the time and never leave."

"We'll stop in every chance we get aight? Right now, you need a little more rest. Come on, let's go."

Once we left the NICU, we told Bonnie and Micah they could go ahead and stop in. On the way to the room, I felt that feeling where I was just at peace. It was weird because I didn't really feel anything else, probably due to me being able to see my babies. I saw Chase and now them. I felt like everything was complete, and as if my work here on earth was done. It brought tears to my eyes because I finally put two and two together. The pain that I was feeling before had left, and that answered my question. I haven't taken any meds in the last four hours and I was due for some here shortly. However, I was numb. I was at ease now and ready to pass on. I knew something was wrong and that broad Nurse Jessica just couldn't follow through on getting me the attention I needed. Now, it's too late.

As he pushed me through the hallways, my vision started to get blurry. I didn't know why God decided to take me right now, especially after the nurse claimed everything was alright. One thing for sure, I hope Chase was smart and took these mafuckas to court. Because I warned that bitch that I wasn't feeling right and she decided to ignore it all because my blood pressure wasn't high. I just knew something was internally fucked up inside of me. I was grateful that I got to name the babies and see them that first and last time. My heart cried out thinking of them living their life without me. I'd always be with them, and I hoped that Chase and Star could make it right and just be together for our family. I know this was gon' break her heart as well as Chase's. Tears started following down my face.

"Cha-chase," I managed to get out as we were almost to my room.

"Yeah, baby?"

"Stop moving and come here," I demanded.

He came around and faced me. He got down so that he could face me, "What's wrong? Why are you crying?"

"Baby, I'm about to leave now, and I want you to take real good care of them, okay? You and Star need to make this right and be together because I'll haunt you if you get with somebody else." I chuckled.

"This not funny, Nookie. What the fuck you mean? AYE, SOMEBODY GET SOME HELP!" He shouted.

"No, Chase, it's over. I'm already slipping away. I don't wanna be resuscitated. So, don't let them do that on me."

"Nookie, no! What the fuck do you mean?" he yelled.

I heard footsteps of somebody running, and I cried even more that meant that Bonnie and Micah were coming up the hallway. Nurses started gathering and rushing to get the materials together for a code blue.

"What's going on?" Bonnie asked.

"She's saying she's gone and she can feel it. She doesn't wanna be brought back once she goes," Chase sobbed.

"Nookie, what? Nooo! What the fuck is taking y'all so long! Get her out of this wheelchair and on a gurney!" Bonnie ordered them.

"Ma'am, she already stated she doesn't wanna be resuscitated, we can't go against that." One of the nurses responded.

"BITCH, WHAT! SHE AIN'T SIGN NO PAPER SAYING THAT SHIT!!!! HELP HER NOW!!!!!!!" Bonnie yelled.

It was too late. I was already going away. I saw the light and all that. I was just grateful I was going to Heaven. I hoped that the people I loved dearly would get their lives right so that we could reunite in the future. Even with all the bs, I went through. It's been a good run, especially these last two years. I wouldn't have it any other way. All I could pray for was that Chase didn't take my death so hard to the point where he couldn't take care of our kids. I hoped this motivated him into being the best father he could ever be. I'd be there to protect them as much as I could.

"I love you," was the last thing I could say before it all went away.

Chapter 34: Micah

Everything that just happened was a blur, and we were all still in awe. Nobody saw this shit turning this way. I was holding Bonnie as she cried, nonstop into my chest. Casino disappeared after they took Nookie away, and I was torn because I didn't wanna leave my girl, but then he was all alone, and he's like a brother to me.

"Come on, let's go," I whispered in her ear.

"I can't, Micah. I can't. Why she didn't tell me that something was wrong?" Bonnie questioned.

"She probably didn't want you to worry. You know Nookie. She's always been selfless."

"A trait that I failed to get. I'm gon' miss her so much."

"Let's go find Casino and make sure he's not doing something crazy." I grabbed her hand, and we went looking around. I called his phone back to back, and he ignored the calls. We went back to where Nookie's room was and immediately heard him yelling.

"I mean, WHAT THE FUCK? So, she told you something was wrong, and you FLAT OUT IGNORED HER?" He was yelling so bad that I could see the veins popping out his neck. We rushed over to his side.

"What happened?" Bonnie asked.

"These mafuckas right here just told me that Nook told her something was wrong. She told her she felt something, and they ignored her."

"Sir, with all due respect, that's not how I meant it. I am truly sorry for your loss, Dr. Graham was in surgery, and that's who Nachelle requested. It was not ignored. She just wasn't readily available," Nurse Jessica responded.

"So, then you should've got somebody else! This is a fucking hospital!" Bonnie screamed at her.

"Please, can you all keep it down? We do have a grieving room, and you all can wait there until Dr. Graham gets here. She can better explain what may have happened to Nachelle," Nurse Rebecca started escorting us to the room.

Once we were in there, it felt like the waiting game.

"This is not over. I swear it ain't. She told me she asked them for help, and they just ignored her. I know they did." Casino was furious. He had his fists balled up, and I could tell he was about to punch a hole through the wall.

"Damn, I have to call Ms. Pam. This is not gon' be good. Micah, how I'mma tell her this?" Bonnie asked me.

"I'll do it if you want me to. I know it won't be easy on you," I replied.

"I'll do it. Ms. Pam needs to hear it coming from me," Casino intervened.

"Okay, bro. You got it. Where is this damn doctor?" I more so asked myself. Within seconds, the doctor was walking in.

"Hello, I am so sorry for your loss, Chase." The doctor walked in and headed in Casino's direction.

"Please stay away from me. I wanna know what happened to my fiancée and why? Why was she even let out of surgery if she wasn't okay?" He started firing questions at her.

"Well, Nachelle was released from surgery because at that time there was nothing wrong. We did not see any alarming factors that occurred from the deliveries," Dr. Graham explained.

"So, what happened then?" Bonnie walked up with her arms folded.

"I'm sensing a lot of hostility in here, and I understand the frustration, I really do, but I cannot comfortably continue to inform you guys of what occurred if I feel threatened."

"Look, Bonnie and Casino chill out. We need to know what happened, and we not gon' find that out when y'all scaring her." They both nodded their heads and took a seat after I spoke.

"Nachelle had a postpartum infection that led to sepsis."

"And what is sepsis?" I questioned.

"It's a deadly inflammatory response to infection. It happened rapidly, which is why she passed on before we could get her on antibiotics," Dr. Graham responded.

"Wow, and she knew something was wrong. She was in pain, and all y'all did was made her wait," Bonnie cried.

"I'm so sorry. I was in surgery. It is protocol that they contact someone else when it's an emergency. I sincerely apologize and will take the proper actions against Nurse Jessica. She advised me she was the one who told Nachelle that I was in surgery."

"If she is not fired by tonight, there will be action taken against this whole damn hospital, and it'll have Nachelle's name on it!" Bonnie yelled and stormed out.

We followed her lead. There was nothing left to say. We had lost someone who was dear to all of us due to the nurse's negligence. If you asked me, Casino and Ms. Pam should be preparing for a major ass lawsuit against St. Vincent Women's Hospital.

***

Nookie's death had put a black cloud around all of us. There was no excitement for wedding plans or even the fact that three beautiful lives were brought into this world. We just wanted her back, but we knew it wouldn't be able to happen. Casino hadn't come out of the house for days. He didn't even visit the babies, according to Ms. Pam, because she had been up there for three days straight now. She and Bonnie were planning Nookie's funeral and made it up in my mind that I would go get Casino ass because I knew he would wanna have some type of say so. I understood that he had just lost the closest person to him, and I knew it'd be hard, but those kids needed him, and Ms. Pam lost her whole daughter and she still made time for her grandchildren. I was headed over to his place now to get him back to himself.

After parking, I walked up to the door, and it was cracked open.

"What the fuck?" I said aloud and pulled out my Glock. The house had a dirty smell to it like old food and sweaty socks. It was dark as hell in here too. I closed the door and locked it then headed to the bedroom. I walked in and shook my head. Casino was sleeping with a bottle of Hennessy in his hand. He had one sock on and one off. My boy was out here doing bad.

"Aye, Casino, Aye!" I shook the bed repeatedly. This nigga wasn't budging.

I went into the bathroom and turned the shower on using cold water only. I knew this nigga was gon' hate me for doing this, but he needed to get his shit together. In one swift motion, I grabbed his arm and placed it around my neck so that I could drag him to the shower.

"W-what the f-fuck?" he said.

"Nigga, to be a small nigga, yo ass is heavy." I laughed, and then once we got in the bathroom, I just threw him into the shower.

"Oh shit!!! This shit cold!!!" he shouted.

"Yeah, I know nigga! What the fuck you think are you doing just letting yo life slip the fuck away. You ain't even seen yo kids', nigga!" I was going off, and he was just looking at me like I was nobody.

"Man, you ain't talking to me like that," he said and turned the shower off, "I do what I want to do when I want to do it."

I followed him as he walked into the bedroom and plopped on the bed.

"Bro, I ain't tryna sound like a naggin' ass mafucka, but Ms. Pam called told me you hadn't been back to the hospital to see them. They already lost their mother. Don't make them lose their father."

"What am I supposed to do? I ain't nothing without Nookie, man. She made me better. How I'mma be a good father without my rock?"

"Man, I ain't gon' sit here and say it'll be okay, or I know what you're going through because I don't truthfully. You already know how I lost it when Bonnie got shot. All I can tell you bro is that we here for you. Whenever you need help or even just a listening ear, we're here. I know it feels like you alone, ESPECIALLY when it comes to the kids, but you're not. We're gon' be there bro, real shit."

I knew Casino was taking in everything I said to him. He just didn't know how to receive it right now. His pride is probably at war with his heart, and I understood 100%.

Sighing heavily, Casino admitted, "I appreciate it, bro. I really do. There's one thing I need to do before I go to the hospital."

"What? Have you talked to CJ?"

"Nah, that's what I need to do, but I have to see Star first. That's one thing Nookie said that she wanted us to remain a family, but how can I when she ain't even here? There will never be another like her."

I could tell he was using all his might not to cry right now. Probably because we were both men, and he didn't wanna look like a bitch.

"Bro, let it out now. I'm your brother. You ain't gotta be embarrassed. You wanna make sure you coo when you relay the news to Star and CJ."

As if he was on cue, he just let it all out. I made sure I stayed there with him, though, because one thing I did know is that if you're alone and so many emotions hit you at once, there's no telling what you'll do then.

Chapter 35: Casino

I never felt any less of a man than how I felt now. I couldn't stop the tears from falling the moment I sat down. From now on, I was just gon' keep myself busy. That's how I knew Nookie was the love of my life. I never shed a tear for no woman. The only time I ever cried was the day my kids were born, CJ and the triplets, but I lost a woman who made me want to be alive, she made me wanna be the best just for her. Now that she was gone, I had no idea how I'd ever be happy again. Star won't be able to fill the void, and I wasn't interested in trying to make her fill it. I know Nookie would want me with Star if I had to be with somebody else, but I didn't care to be with anybody else.

I pulled up to Ms. Pam's house to pick up CJ and prepared myself for the lecture I knew she was about to give me. Walking inside the house, my stomach growled at the smell of her amazing cooking. I smelled fried chicken, collard greens, macaroni and cheese, and there was a sweet smell, but I couldn't put my finger on it. I entered the kitchen, and she was dancing to an old school song that I didn't even know. I turned the radio off.

"Boy, don't touch my radio, you crazy?" She swatted my hand away and turned it back on.

"Ms. Pam, I need to talk to you." I turned it back off.

"Chase, I have been crying all morning, I don't wanna start back." Ms. Pam gripped the sides of the sink.

"I know because I have too. I came to apologize to you for everything."

"Ohhhh Chase, have a seat, I don't blame you for anything. So, please don't feel that way." She came over and gave me the warmest hug. I started to slide back into that depression but was able to back out of it once CJ ran in.

"Daddy!!!" He gripped my leg, and I picked him up and gave him the biggest hug.

"Wassup, lil man! You been having fun with Granny Pam?"

"Yes! And she bought me a hot wheel track!" CJ shouted with excitement.

"She did? Did you tell her thank you?" I questioned.

"Yes, he did. He always does." Ms. Pam rubbed his head and smiled.

"Go ahead and play until it's time to go," I ordered.

He ran back into the living room. Ms. Pam and I both took a seat at the table, and she grabbed my hand.

"You know I was a little disappointed in you not being active at the hospital for these first couple of days."

"Wel— "

I was about to talk, but then she held her hand up.

"Let me finish, I was angry, I wanted to call you every name in the book, but then I had to take a step back and re-evaluate myself. You lost your soul mate, your rib, the apple to your eye, and not only that, but you watched her take her last breath. I know it would've hurt even more coming there this soon."

"Ms. Pam."

"Call me mama, Chase."

"Mama, it's not even that. I mean, you're right. It'll be like opening a wound all over again, but it's the fact that I don't how to look my babies in the face knowing I failed them. I couldn't protect their mother, so how I'mma protect them? Nookie literally made me better, and she didn't even know she was doing it."

"I know, son. Trust me. She has saved me more times than she knew. But, you know what? She knows how much you loved her, and she trusts that you'll do right by them. She's looking over all of us and will continue to do so. I feel her all the time. I just ask that you don't give up because CJ needs you and so does the triplets." Ms. Pam started wiping her eyes.

"I got you, ma. I'll do right by Nookie and try my best." The smell hit my nose again, and at this point, my stomach was gon' beat my ass if I ain't feed it, "Can I please get a plate? My stomach is over here crying."

We started laughing as she made my plate. I was happy as hell because the sweet scent I smelled was sweet potato pie. I ate so much food and planned to take a nap before CJ, and I had to go and see Star.

***

I held CJ hand as we waited for Star to come out. The double doors opened, and she ran out and hugged us both.

"Hey, mommy!" CJ shouted.

"Hey, my baby! I missed you so much!" Star planted kisses all over his face. "Hey, Chase."

"How you doing?" I asked.

"It's going okay. One day at a time, I was gon' call y'all, but they said for the first couple of weeks, we needed to focus on ourselves."

"No need to explain anything to me. If this place is really working for you, you won't hear too much kickback from me."

"Where's Nookie?" Star inquired.

"That's actually why we had to come see you in person. I have to tell you something." I tried my best to keep a poker face. I didn't wanna lead her into relapsing. That's why I had to give her the information here because she'd already be in an environment that she could get help if she needed it. We went inside and sat on the bench in the lobby.

"Chase, what's going on why you so serious?"

"Look, Nookie had the babies three months early. They are premature and in the NICU at St. Vincent Women's Hospital."

"What? Oh my god, is Nookie okay? I know she's going insane about that," Star expressed.

"Star, Nookie died after surgery."

"Boy, gon' on somewhere. I know you lying."

"Would I really come all the way down here and tell you that just to be lying? CJ doesn't even know."

"Chaseeeeee, oh my goddd!" Star just started crying uncontrollably. I put my arms around her and let her cry in my arms.

"Daddy, what's wrong with mommy?" CJ asked me.

"You know Miss Nachelle? We won't be seeing her anymore. So, we need to be strong for your mommy and your new brothers and sister," I explained to him.

"I'm sad now, daddy. I love Miss Nachelle." CJ started poking his lip out, and that broke my heart. However, I needed to let them know. The funeral was in a few days, and I wanted to give Star more than enough time to decide what she wanted to do.

"I gotta go," Star said as she rose up from the bench.

"You gon' be okay?"

"I will be."

"Do you need me to tell them you need a meeting or session?" I was serious as hell. I didn't want her to mess up.

"No, Chase, I will be fine. Just let me know when the funeral arrangements are," Star demanded before she dispersed inside the building.

"Daddy, will mommy be going away too?" CJ looked up at me.

"No, son, she'll be coming back with us soon. I can promise you that."

Chapter 36: Bonnie

Ms. Pam and I were in the middle of my living room, trying to get all the information gathered for Nookie's obituary.

"Dang, so Nookie was doing your hair at the age of 11?" I asked her.

"Girl yeah, she was bomb at an early age. She knew off the top that she wanted to be a hairstylist. Do you know how many Barbie dolls she had filled with braids?" she chuckled.

"I can imagine. Man, Nookie stayed making sure my hair was on fleek. I'mma miss the hell out of her man."

My mind started drifting, and I needed to keep busy before I started crying again. My stomach felt very uneasy, and I didn't know why because I didn't eat anything yet. Suddenly, a rush of sickness came over me, and I ran to the bathroom throwing up all the bile that was in my stomach since I ain't ate shit. I heard Ms. Pam walking up to the bathroom.

"You okay, baby?"

"Yes, ma'am, it's just a little sickness from crying," I said back.

"Okay, let me know if you need anything. I'm gonna go give this information over to the lady so she can make sure the obituaries are ready. If yo fine ass daddy come by tell him to leave them young whippersnappers alone and come see what the cougars are about." She laughed.

I gagged in the toilet.

"O-ok!" I shouted so she could get the gist to go head and go. Once I was done, I cleaned myself up and went into the bedroom to change my shirt.

I grabbed my phone, and my daddy hadn't called. That was weird because since he found out the news, he had been on my line every day, I was able to talk to him since Nookie died but haven't seen him. Now it was going on two days since we spoke.

I put on one of Micah t-shirts just in case I had to throw up again, I didn't have to get it on my shit. It just blew my mind how I got sick like that. I went to the OBGYN last month, and she didn't mention pregnancy or anything, so I was confused.

Walking into the living room, my heart fell in my stomach. I was cursing myself out because I left the pistol in the bedroom. I did have my phone though, just in case I needed to call Micah.

"Who the fuck are you?" I questioned.

"So, this is where you live, huh? Bonnie Jones, infamous queen pin, murderer, and money launderer," the man spoke nonchalantly.

"I ain't gon' ask again."

"I'm sorry we haven't met yet. Yo hubby or almost hubby met me a couple of months ago."

"So, you the dirty cop?"

"Dirty is such a strong word. I like to call it as being an opportunist. I see my chance and take it."

"Well, whatever you fucking do, why are you in my shit? Like do you know I can kill you easily and get away with it due to you trespassing?"

This mafucka done lost his rabbit ass mind thinking he's gon' walk up in here like that.

"Oh, I know what you're capable of, but you'd be making a dumb ass decision. I got some information you may want." He started talking and then my phone rang.

"Lemme take this call, what was your name? Nah, never mind. It doesn't matter I'mma call you jackass." I snickered as I answered the phone.

"Hello?"

"Hey, Bonnie, it's me Don."

"Hey, Don, is there anything going on? I know the hearing isn't set for another two weeks."

"Nope, nothing is going on other than the charges have been dropped! The DA can't proceed with the case."

Jumping up and down in excitement, I screamed, "Are you forreal?"

"Yes, Bonnie, it's all over. They couldn't locate the undercover cop's whereabouts, and no new evidence surfaced. You are good to go."

"Thank you so much, Don, for everything. I'll wire you the money in the morning."

As soon as I said that, I regretted it as I hung up the phone. I forgot the jackass was here.

"Sounds like you got some good news, and the name is Roland." He chuckled.

"I definitely did. The case is closed. I'm officially a free woman."

"For now. You see, if you don't do what I say or make it worth my while, I guess I should say, I'm gonna alert them about your trip out of the country, which is a felony. You were technically still held to the obligations of an inmate. You just weren't in jail. Oh, and I have Reaper's murder on record." He smiled.

"I don't know what you're talking about," I replied. He wouldn't dare get any type of confession from me.

"Oh, really?" Roland took out an old recorder.

"Who even uses those anymore it's 2019?"

"Shit, I ain't do it. Sniper's ass sent it to me."

"That mafucka," I mumbled under my breath.

He played the recording, and I shook my head. This mafucka somehow bugged my place. My mind started racing trying to figure out when he could have done it. I guess it really didn't matter seeing that he was gone.

"So, what now? You have that information. What do you want?" I questioned.

"I wanna quit my job, and in order to do that, I need enough money to make sure my family can live comfortably."

"And how much are you talking?"

"One million dollars." This nigga said it as if he was asking for ten dollars.

"Ha, you a damn lie," I responded.

"What's a million dollars to you? What about your investments? You should be making more than that by now."

"What I make is none of your concern. Your concern should be your life. You don't know anything about me other than what a mafucka can pull on MyCase, so stop acting as if you do. You're nothing but a damn rent-a-cop compared to the real mafuckas like the FEDS. Your best bet would be to take this $100,000 that I have on me right now and leave the recorder behind, or you won't have a family to live a comfortable life for." With each word I spoke, Roland's eyes got bigger. I needed him to hear the venom in my voice. "I just lost my best friend four days ago, and I won't hesitate on any more actions, I need for you to leave, now."

He just stood there staring at me. I started feeling uncomfortable because he was really a creep. I could tell just by looking at him.

"You know, I think I may take you up on the offer. Now, don't think you hoed me because remember, I'M the one with the badge. I could easily kill you and not think twice about it."

"Oh, shut the hell up, you won't hurt a damn fly."

I laughed and headed to the bedroom to grab the duffel bag that was filled with money. I went to my nightstand and grabbed my .9mm and put it in my waistband just in case this mafucka even thought he was gon' try me.

I returned to the living room and threw it at his feet, I watched as he bent down to grab the bag, and then I pulled out my gun and aimed at his head. He rose up, and his eyes almost popped out his head.

"Wait, come on now, I thought we were better than that." Even when this mafucka got a gun to his face, he's still on creep mode.

"I just want you to know I'm not playing with you. If you EVER think about coming to my house again, there will be no questions asked. Leave the recorder and get the fuck out."

I watched him as he pulled the recorder out his pocket and threw it at my feet. He slowly made his way to the door and then stopped.

"You know you lucky you so damn fine or else I'd take this money and still turn yo ass in. But, seeing that I'll enjoy seeing you around the way, I'm not gon' do that." He smirked.

"Oh please, yo dried up Ace Hood looking ass needs to get the fuck up outta here. You ain't crazy. You know your family will be gone tomorrow. Now step," I demanded. He made his exit, and I rolled my eyes. It was always something. Hopefully, that was my first and last time seeing his ass.

I didn't even know whether or not to tell Micah. I'm opting out of that. He doesn't need to know because I handled it. I promise once I say, "I do," I won't keep anything else from him. There's no need for any more negative energy to be placed upon us. I had to prepare myself for tomorrow. I was laying my best friend to rest forever, and my heart broke at the thought of that. I would try my best to be strong for all of them because Lord knows I done cried and cried until my eyes became sore. I never thought I wouldn't have a maid of honor at my wedding. No one can replace her, so I'll just be by myself. One thing for sure was her funeral would be beautiful, and we were going to celebrate the life of Nachelle Hughes.

***

There I stood, in front of my best friend lying in a casket. I made sure she was decked out in the finest brand of clothing. We chose a pink Prada bejewelled Crepe cady dress that showed off her beautiful collarbone. They were able to get on a nice pair of black flats. Her hair was flowing, and she looked so beautiful. Sprowl Funeral Home did an amazing job on my best friend. Ms. Pam and I had on the same dress Nookie wore. Ours was just in black. I bought us pair of Christian Louboutin heels with the sunglasses to match. I couldn't allow anyone to see my eyes today. I was bound to go nuts. I kissed her forehead, and Micah placed his hand on my lower back. He directed me to the front row. I stopped in front of Ms. Pam and hugged her.

"I love you, thank you so much for all this." She rocked me back and forth, and I felt her tears hitting my shoulder.

"I love you too. And you already know I wouldn't have had it any other way."

Micah and I took a seat next to Ms. Pam. I looked around because Casino hadn't walked up yet, he, Star, and CJ were in the back of the funeral car with us, so I'm not sure where they are. This was only a small funeral, so there weren't many people here. I took my eyes off her casket once, and when I looked back, I almost got whiplash. This bitch had the audacity to show up here. I would turn-up if this wasn't a special occasion.

I can't even be mad, though, because she was Nookie's friend. She just better hoped my daddy didn't wring her neck once he showed up. I cringed as she walked over to us and told us that she was sorry for our loss. Somebody must've told her when I put the funeral arrangements on my Facebook. I prepared myself to get through the next two hours.

Chapter 37: Casino

I sat in the back of the car and felt numb as hell. It's just as if I couldn't move. I could hear Star in my ear, begging me to come on because she didn't want to come in alone.

"Chase, please come on. We have to get in there before they close the casket."

"Then go Star. Do you understand what I'm going through right now?"

"Yes, I do. She wasn't just important to you, Chase!" Star opened the door, "Come on, CJ." He grabbed her hand, and they headed inside the church. I felt like shit because she was right. I got out of the car and started walking up to the church.

"Aye!" somebody yelled. I looked over, and it was OG and Mercedes.

"Wassup, OG?" I said somberly.

"Why you not in there already, youngblood?"

"I just can't believe this shit is happening forreal."

"I already know, man, but you gotta be strong. One thing you'll regret is not being there before they close that casket." He patted me on the shoulder, and then they walked in.

I followed them as we walked into the sanctuary. She always said she was gon' start going back to church. With each step, it felt like I was dragging my feet. OG and Mercedes paid their respects, and then it was my turn. The whole room grew quiet. I went into my pocket and pulled out the pink ring box that I was saving for our anniversary. Now, all I was left with were regrets.

"I didn't think this would happen, Nook. I just knew we were gon' be laid up happy as hell right now planning our anniversary." I put the ring box in the cup of her arm and kissed her forehead. I was about to walk away, but a wave of emotions hit me.

"Nook really? Like we had big ass plans, and you left me. I know I sound selfish as hell, but you just left me all alone. You made me fall in love with you and then bounced. What I'm supposed to tell the kids when they ask why everybody got a mama and they don't?"

I couldn't believe I was crying again. I guess because this was the final time I'd be able to see her face. This shit was worse than any pain I could imagine. I felt somebody place their hand on my shoulder. I looked, and it was Micah.

"Come on, bro," he said.

"Nah, I ain't staying. I can't do this. I gotta go." I snatched away from him and left the church. I just started walking. I didn't care where I was going. I just couldn't stay.

***

I smiled as I held Cairo in my arms. He was getting very attached to me, and I knew he felt that I was his father. I'd been here since I left the church, and I was happy I came here because my babies were doing great. They were progressing very quickly according to the doctor. She even said once they hit six pounds, they could be released. Of course, my boys were excelling quicker than Nadia, but I have a feeling she gon' get her mother's strength and her weight will shoot up. I put Cairo back into his incubator and walked out of the NICU to grab a cup of coffee.

"Now, how did I know this where you were gon' be?" Micah asked.

"Damn nigga, you persistent ain't you?" I snarled.

"I'm making sure yo ass don't go off the deep end, plus Bonnie made me come." He laughed.

"Aww yeah, I guess you had better come then. She got yo ass wrapped around her finger. I can't imagine how it's gon' be when y'all get married." I laughed back.

"Shut up, nigga, she knows what it is. How are you holding up?"

"I'm good, and I really don't wanna get into all the deep shit right now. My babies are gaining their weight and will be able to come home soon, so I'm tryna stay excited about that."

"I understand, bruh."

It got quiet, so I decided to break the silence.

"So, you ready for the big day?"

"What? The wedding? Shit, that's if she wanna continue it right now."

"Nigga, it's two weeks away, I'm pretty sure she wanna marry yo ass if she ain't cancel it by now." I took off the jacket to the suit I was wearing.

"I'm just ready to get it done. It seems like something bad happens every time we get closer and closer. I should've taken her offer on eloping, so that way, Nookie would've at least been a part of it."

"Damn. But, y'all gon' have a good wedding bro because you know Nookie she wouldn't have let nobody ruin that day for Bonnie, not even her."

"I already know, bro."

"There y'all are," I heard Bonnie say.

"Shit," was the first thing I could say. I knew Bonnie was probably gon' be shitty that I walked out on the funeral like that, and then I looked, and she brought Star ass too.

"Wassup, where's CJ?" I tried to steer the subject away from me before they started.

"Nah, don't try to deflect, why would you leave like that Chase? Star put her hands on her hips.

"Star, I'm not tryna get into all that. I'm really not."

"I understand what you did, Casino. You have no judgment from me, that's for sure."

Bonnie went and took a seat next to Micah. Star just threw her hands up to surrender. She out of all people should know that I ain't gon' be bullied into thinking what I did was wrong, and I stood on that.

"How are the babies?" Bonnie asked.

"They're doing great. The doctor says they should be able to be released fairly soon," I replied.

"Aww, that's so good. Cause I would like for them to be at the wedding. Hopefully, they're released before then. I already have a seat that's gon' be dolled up and reserved for Nookie."

"That's wassup. You know I'm probably gon' need a little of help these first couple of months that they're home," I mentioned it to everybody, but I was more so directing that comment to Star. She looked up and looked around to make sure I'm talking to her. I started laughing, "Yeah, girl, I'm talking to you too."

"Does that mean you want me to move back in?"

"I mean, yeah. That way CJ could always have access to both of us. I mean with the new position I'm in, I'mma need somebody to hold the home front down. Nookie went all out with making sure that house is where it's at, and I don't wanna be the one messing that up," I explained.

"Nigga, you damn near already did." Micah chuckled.

Giving him the finger, I voiced, "That was a slip up I got shit under control now. I just wanna make sure I get the shit right, and I know it takes a village or whatever that damn saying is. Losing Nookie was my weakest moment, but I'm no longer in that mindset.

After hearing my kids are almost home, I gotta realize I'mma man, and I can't let them see me fold."

"Aight then shit, we got you, bro. You know we support you." Micah came up and shook up with me.

Star came over to my side. "100%."

I gave her a small hug, and for the rest of the night, we just took turns checking on the kids and sharing memories of Nookie. I knew she'd always be a part of me. No other woman would be able to fill the void I was missing. I made sure not to get Star's hopes up because she has always been the one to fall for a nigga so easily. I was mentally preparing for the takeover that was about to happen. I knew it wouldn't be easy gaining all the trust from Bonnie's henchmen, the people she supplied, and the overall crew of people who helped Bonnie get to where she is now. However, I did know one thing for sure, if they had a problem with the new boss, they could get ghost quick.

Chapter 38: OG

"Now before we start, are you sure this is what you want to do?" the doctor clarified with me for the 100th time.

"Yes, doc, as I told you before, my daughter already lost someone else dear to her. I can't be the third person who's taken away from her. If I could at least try to then if I don't succeed, at least she'd know I tried my best."

After Nookie passed, I decided to go to the doctor to ask to start chemo. My baby girl deserved for me to at least try to get better. I was adamant about not receiving any treatment, but I had to put her first. I wanted to be around if she had children. Another thing I took into consideration was that Mercedes and I were really enjoying each other. I know I couldn't really compare the two, but she was so much like Malorie. Bonnie's mother supported me 100% and always catered to me, and that's what I got from Mercedes. She wasn't a woman who expected material things because she could provide them for her damn self. She wasn't interested in playing games or being childish when it came to showing how she felt, and I appreciated that.

"I'm so proud of you, babe. I'll be right out here in the waiting room." Mercedes kissed me on the lips. Once she left, I closed my eyes and prepared to get this shit started.

***

"The first session went pretty well," the doctor said to me.

"Yeah, well, it doesn't feel that way. I ain't even gon' lie to you."

"That's a normal reaction to the chemo. Your body is not used to this type of treatment, especially when it's at this level of aggression due to the state of the cancer."

"I hear you loud and clear, doc. I'll see you next week for my next round." I extended my hand, and he shook it.

I walked out of the lab and saw Mercedes sleeping on the couch in the waiting room. I walked over to her and ran my hand through her hair. She started waking up and smiled once she noticed it was me.

"How'd it go, papi?"

"It went like I thought it would. I feel horrible."

"My poor baby, he did say that that the Nexavar would have some irritable side effects."

"It'll all be worth it if it's helping. This would all be for nothing if the cancer isn't going anywhere."

"Well, Darryl, you still have time if you want to change your mind," Mercedes stated.

"Yeah, I know, but I made a decision to try. I feel like if Bonnie loses anybody else, she will go back to that cold-hearted woman she used to be. And right now, she's in a very good space, and I don't wanna fuck that up."

"I understand. I truly do. I just want you to know that I'm gon' support you, regardless."

I grabbed her by the waist and took her into my arms.

"I know." I embraced her tightly, "So, do you think I should share this news with Bonnie now or maybe it could be a wedding gift."

"I think you should tell her now. It'd bring the wedding more joy than ever."

"Yeah, and I don't wanna take away the importance from her on that day. I say we all have dinner tonight, and then I'll tell them then."

"Sounds good, papi. I'll text her and see if they're free."

Mercedes started folding up the little blanket she asked for since she was always cold. When she turned up, she looked at me as if she saw a ghost.

"What's wrong?"

"Your nose, it's bleeding like a lot."

"Fucking random nose bleeds." I cursed aloud. She grabbed the box of Kleenex and I held my head back. She made sure she wiped my nose and stuffed some tissue up my right nostril.

"Okay, no, I'm worried now." Mercedes sat down and put her face in her hands.

"Look, I thank you for being strong throughout this process because you don't have to be here with me through it." I sat next to her and grabbed her hands.

"I know Darryl, but I wanna be, and I know this is all new to not just me but for you too. If it's helping, I know this will be worth it. Now, enough of this, let's go tell Bonnie." She smiled, and I felt ten times better. That's all that a nigga needed sometimes, the confirmation from his woman that everything would be alright.

***

"You ready?" Mercedes asked me as we waited outside Bonnie's door.

"As ready as I can be," I replied and then rang the doorbell. A minute went by before Micah opened the door.

"Wassup, youngblood?" I reached out my hand, and he hesitated before grabbing my hand and pulling me in for a hug.

Breaking the hug, he quizzed, "You doing alright, OG?"

"You know what, I am. I'll tell y'all more about it once we gather at the table."

Micah stepped aside so that Mercedes and I could enter, "And what about you? You doing okay?"

"Yes, thank you for asking," she responded.

"Bonnie! Pops and Mercedes are here," he announced, and then he dispersed into the kitchen.

A part of me was happy, yet, surprised that he called me pops. I'm glad he was able to put the bullshit aside for Bonnie because I wanted her to have the best life she could from this point on, and that included all of us.

"Hey, daddy." She came out looking just like her mother.

"Wassup baby girl, how's everything going?" I hugged her, and we headed to the dinner table.

"Everything's going great. I just finished up my vows, and hopefully, Micah did the same seeing that the wedding is approaching soon."

Micah said nothing. He just shrugged his shoulders, and we all burst out laughing.

"What you cook?"

Giggling, Bonnie commented, "I knew the question was coming, but I have baked chicken smothered in gravy, fried cabbage with sausages, sweet potatoes, and I made a pecan pie."

"You in here cooking like your mother. You made all of that in six hours?" I questioned.

"Yes, well, I started last night. Micah said he wanted a home-cooked meal, and I haven't been able to cook since all that's happened."

"Her cooking gon' get you bigger, youngblood."

Laughing, Micah voiced, "I already know that's why I'mma have to build a gym in her basement."

"Yeah, cause I'mma need that eight-pack to stay right." Bonnie cracked up. "Let's eat, y'all."

Micah and I took a seat as Bonnie and Mercedes made the plates. They had a bottle of red wine chilling in ice. Bonnie was her mother's child. She loved red wine. Micah popped open the bottle and filled everyone's glass. Once our plates were in front of us, as I prayed over the food, we all held hands.

"Dear Lord, I ask that you bless the food and the hands that prepared it. May it be nourishing to our bodies and continue to bring us together. I thank you for my daughter and for the life you have in store for us from now on. Lord, I pray that you continue to provide a shield over us and we continue to prosper. In Jesus' name, I pray, Amen." I let go of Mercedes and Bonnie's hand and began digging in.

"Daddy, that prayer was strong. You had a pastor's voice going on there." She laughed.

"Well, I just got a lot to be grateful for. I have some good news." I wiped my mouth with the napkin. "I know that everything seems like it's been a battle or that our lives are going downhill. Bonnie, back in Cuba, I told you about the cancer diagnoses, and I know it took a toll on you and then to come back home and lose your best friend, I know that was even harder. I'm sorry I couldn't shield you from all of that. Hopefully, my decision to start treatment can help ease some of your pain." As I was speaking, I saw tears coming from Bonnie's eyes.

"Are you serious?" she asked me.

"Yes. I did my first treatment earlier today."

"Thank you so much!" She got up and ran over to hug me.

I held my baby girl tight in my arms. This was what I was looking forward to and couldn't just give that up. I would do everything in my power to remain on this earth until my body just can't do it anymore. One thing nobody will be able to say is that I didn't try hard enough.

Chapter 39: Micah

Today was the day. I was marrying my better half. I never expected that we'd get this far. This has been one hell of a bumpy road, and we have made many sacrifices to please the other.

Nevertheless, those are the signs that made me know that Bonnie was the woman for me. I needed someone who matched the same energy, someone who I looked at as my equal, and that was Bonnie. I really took into consideration if my love for her would be stronger than me wanting kids, and it was. Bonnie didn't wanna tell me, but something had to be up. Either she couldn't have kids, or the Lord was waiting for us to be married first. Either way, I was picking her. Of course, I opted out of having a bachelor party, and Casino wasn't feeling up to it anyway. That's my best man, so if he didn't wanna have bitches all in his face, I damn sure didn't.

I stared at myself in the mirror as I fixed my tie. I looked over to Casino, and he was doing the same thing. Versace made our tuxedos. Our jackets were white with gold specks throughout and white slacks to match. On our feet were all white Medusa Belt Loafers. The tie was gold with the cufflinks to match. I had to say I looked good as fuck. I knew my baby was gon' match my fly. I hadn't seen her since the dinner we had with her father. I was anxious as fuck.

"Bro, I gotta say, we clean up nice. I'm happy for you, bro." Casino patted me on the shoulder.

"Right on, you know, if you need any time to step away from all of this, I understand." I couldn't help but think about how he might be hurt by all this knowing he was supposed to be walking down the aisle with his fiancée.

"Bro, I'm good. Nookie will be with me in spirit. This is about you and Bonnie. I do have a surprise, though."

"What is it?"

"Ms. Pam will be bringing it before the ceremony starts, so it'll be in the audience."

We looked at ourselves in the mirror and saw that everything was complete. Then, someone knocked at the door. I made my way over and saw that it was OG.

"Wassup, youngblood? Look at you niggas!" He came in cracking up. "I can't believe it. This is really happening."

"Yeah, who would've thought Bonnie would even let a nigga get close to her and now look." I shook my head as I said those words. She gave a nigga hell at first, but I already knew I had her on lock.

"Wait, lemme fix your tie. It's crooked," OG said as he came over and moved it a little to the left.

"Right on, I appreciate that. Well, it's time."

I reached for the knob, and my palms got sweaty. I didn't really have cold feet up until this moment. What if Bonnie decided she ain't wanna marry a nigga no more and left me at the altar? All the cockiness I was feeling started dwindling away. That was until OG grabbed my shoulders for me to face him.

"Look, the feeling you are having right now is not a surprise. Every man feels that before he decides to be with someone that he hopes will be for the rest of his life. Forever is a long-time son. However, I can see in you and Bonnie's eyes that y'all are meant to be. I know we had our bullshit, but I'm here to tell you that you are my son-in-law, and Bonnie is your soul mate."

The words he said to me almost had a nigga shed a tear. "Thank you for that, forreal. I don't know why it just hit me out of nowhere. I was so ready two minutes ago."

"It's all good. Just take a minute to relax, and then we move when you do. I'mma have to go by Bonnie's room so that I can walk her down the aisle."

"I already know. Go handle that, OG." He headed out the room, and I looked over at Casino.

"Aight, I think I'm ready."

"Lead the way." Casino added.

***

I arrived at the entrance of the walkway and saw a pretty good amount of people from both sides of our families waiting for the ceremony to begin.

"You ready, Micah? The music should be starting here shortly," Ms. Jane mentioned.

"Yes, I'm ready," I replied.

"Okay, best man, you'll be walking directly behind him. Good luck, you guys." She cheesed as she made her way inside of the banquet hall.

Ms. Jane truly had the Ballare Ballroom Events Center decked out. The gold and white setting was the shit, and I was proud of Bonnie for choosing Ms. Jane. She treated us like royalty and would be compensated appropriately.

The doors opened, and I started walking down the white walkway that had gold rose petals sprinkled on it with Casino in tow. We didn't have a flower girl, only a ring bearer.

Once we made it to our spots, I turned and faced everyone. I saw Miguel, Rich, and even that little nigga Chico, a lot of Bonnie's henchmen were here. My hittas were in the building, so it was about to be a celebration. I felt like some of the people were just fans of ours from our Instagram page. I barely even recognized them. I looked on Bonnie's side, and there was a chair reserved for her mother and then one for Nookie. It was decked out in a sheer white dressing with a bouquet of roses on each seat. I looked on my side and there was one for my mother as well.

I got goosebumps once I heard the beginning of the song that was about to play. It was the intro to "The Matrimony" by Wale and Usher.

"Getting engaged is like getting, uh, it's the first hill of the roller coaster, and you hear those clickers, the loud sound – this

really violent, metal 'Chunka-chunka-chunka' and you go, "What, what's going on here?" You know?

"Boy, this thing is really, really goes high!"

And then you go over the top, the wedding is at the top. You go over the top, is the wedding and then you're just screaming, No, it's uh, it's like any growth. You're no- you can't be ready for it because tha- it's growth, it's gonna be new. It's gonna be new. You're gonna have a new life, you're gonna be a new person."

While he spoke, CJ walked down the aisle with the rings on a little white pillow. He was dressed in his little tux that matched mine and Casino's. His smile brightened up the entire room. I was anxious and nervous at the same time. I couldn't wait to see how my baby looked in her dress. Everybody rose, and I could barely see her figure at the beginning of the aisle.

"If there's a question of my heart, you've got it, it don't belong to anyone, but you. If there's a question of my love, you've got it, baby don't worry I've got plans for you."

As Usher sang the lyrics to our favorite song, Bonnie and OG slowly made their way down the aisle. The dress fit her body perfectly. I couldn't wait to reveal the most beautiful face that I would be able to wake up to every morning. A rush of emotions came over me, and before I knew it, I was crying. I refused to wipe my tears because this was happiness for me. Bonnie is the love of my life, and I was grateful to God for putting me in her life. She made that beautiful smile that caused me to fall in love with her in the first place. You could hear everyone commenting on how beautiful she looked throughout the crowd. The dress hit every curve perfectly. I ran my hand across the waves on top of my head and gave her a look of admiration. I wanted to lay her down right now in the dress and all.

"But, I'm promising you better though, and your friends saying let him go, and we ain't getting any younger, I can give up now, but I can promise you forever though, that's right."

The ending of verse one was my signal to approach Bonnie and her father. The moment we all been waiting

Chapter 40: Bonnie

* Ten minutes before the ceremony began*

I stared at myself in the mirror, admiring the beautiful dress that was inspired by my mother's wedding dress. My shoulders were shining bright as the white lace pressed against my skin. My silhouette was perfectly curved, and then it flowed out at the bottom. I didn't have a ridiculously long train because I never understood the point of them.

I heard a soft knock at the door, and it was Ms. Jane.

"Hey, look who I ran into in the hallway." She moved to the side and in walked my daddy.

"Hi, daddy." I smiled.

"Baby girl, you look beautiful. Why you didn't tell me you were using Ms. Jane?" he asked.

"I wanted it to be a surprise, just like the dress. Mama's dress inspired mine." I watched as he scanned me over.

"It sure is. Wow, thank you so much for that, baby girl." We hugged, and I squeezed him tightly. "Aight baby girl, I ain't going nowhere. You know this chemo got me fragile as hell." He laughed.

"That's not funny, daddy. You gon' make me start crying and mess up my makeup."

"You barely got any on wit ya big head ass. You don't need all of that anyway."

"I know, but this is my wedding day, which is why I just had them do my eyes and lips. Daddy, I'm nervous." I sat on the stool and put my bouquet down on the vanity stand.

"I know you are. It's normal. Let you in on a little secret, Micah's feeling the nerves too."

"He is? Whew, because I was over here feeling bad for even having cold feet."

"As I told him, it's normal, and y'all are meant to be together, I saw with my own eyes and you wanna know who else told me so?"

"Who?"

"Your mother."

"You talked to my mama? In your dreams or something?" I questioned.

"Nah, she came to me in person. It was probably because I was doing a lot of comparing between her and Mercedes. She came to me and let me know that she's okay and that Mercedes is perfect for me."

"Wow, I didn't know that. I wish she would come to me. I miss her so much."

"I know you do. When you look into the audience, I want you to see the surprise that's out there for you." He wrapped his arm around my shoulder and planted a kiss on top of my head. He grabbed the tiara-like veil and placed it on top of my head. It was gold studded and sheer.

"Come on, you ready to marry your soulmate?" He held his arm out for me to connect my arm with his.

"More than ever."

***

"Who gives this bride away today?" Pastor Ramsey asked.

"I do," my daddy said and kissed me on the cheek. He connected hands with Micah and nodded his head.

Tears were flowing down my face the moment I saw them flowing down his. He took his thumb and wiped my mascara and my tears from under my eyes, and I wiped his tears from his face.

"Per the bride and groom's request, they would like to read their vows first. Bride, you're up."

I started shaking a little. I was so nervous that I may stumble over my words.

"Micah, my Micah, I never knew anybody would ever get me to settle down, especially not through marriage." The crowd laughed, and so did we. "You already know how hardheaded I am when it comes to love, and I appreciate all the patience that you've given to me. I want to apologize here, in front of all our loved ones for the times that I've walked out on you. You didn't deserve that."

"Wait, you ain't about to leave me at this altar, are you?" He was serious as hell. The crowd gasped.

"Hell no boy, oh, I'm sorry, Pastor."

"You know, for some reason, this just tells me that y'all were destined to be together. Continue, Bonnie." Pastor Ramsey chuckled.

"I promise from here on out that I will always come to you first about how I feel and remain true to our love. I promise that I will forever be your listening ear and treat you how a king is supposed to be treated. I thank you for changing my heart from coldness to a heart full of love. Thank you for being my protector and making me feel secure at all times. You are the love of my life, my everything, my better half, and the man that will always be known to get Bonnie to submit. I don't how you were able to do it, but I guess I'm hypnotized by a savage. I love you, Micah Walker, to the death of me."

He was smiling hard as hell. I couldn't do my vows without having a little ghetto part in it. That's just me, I may be bougie at times, but you gon' get the ghetto Bonnie every now and then.

"You gotta forgive me. You know I'm not all that good at expressing myself, so hopefully, these vows will display how you make me feel. I never thought I'd ever be able to love another woman until I met you. You blew my mind the first day we met, literally showing me that you're my match before we even shared a dialogue with one another. I could see that you were hurt in the past, and I made it my mission to correct the last man's wrongs. I promise to always be your provider, your knight in shining armor, and your shoulder to lean on. I thank you for being there for me through the ups and downs and for making sure that I am always satisfied. There's nothing you can do that or anything anyone can ever say to steer my love in another direction. I love you and only you and will always remain loyal to you. I pray that God continues to keep me in your life, and I think he knows how reckless we both can get any time we're not together. So, it's only right that we stay solid and continue rocking with each other forever." Micah kissed the tear that was falling down my face.

"Can he kiss the bride now?" I asked Pastor. He just gave me a stern look, and the crowd burst in laughter again.

As we proceeded through the ceremony, I said I do, and so did he. We exchanged rings and lit the single candle at the same time. Our love was united, and I was happy we were arriving at the moment I've been waiting for.

"I hereby announce Mr. and Mrs. Micah Walker! You may kiss the bride," Pastor Ramsey said.

Micah grabbed the sides of my head and our lips connected. It felt so magnetic this time around. We kissed all the time, but now that we were married, it felt much more passionate. We finally parted and joined hands. We walked down the aisle, and everyone was congratulating us. That's when we noticed who was in the crowd on my side.

"Ms. Pam? Are those the babies? Oh my god!" I shouted. They were all three asleep in their car seats. They were peaceful and looked so comfortable. I couldn't wait until the reception so that I could hold my precious god babies. I had no idea that they were already home, and the fact that they were here celebrating with us made it all better, especially with them representing their mama. We continued expressing our thanks to everyone before we headed out to take pictures.

***

It was time for the reception, and this would be the highlight of the night. I couldn't wait to see everyone and dance all night long.

"Again, welcome Mr. and Mrs. Micah Walker!"

We danced our way in as "No Chill" by Wale and Jeremih played. We were huge fans of Wale, so we were feeling ourselves. My daddy, Mercedes, Ms. Pam, Casino, Star, CJ, and the triplets were all waiting for us. We took our seats at the long table that was at the front of the room. We were still at the Ballare Ballroom Events Center. We just used a separate room for the reception. Famous Dave's catered all the food and our cake was custom made by Gigi's Bakery. Everyone was eating and having an overall good time. I stood up and tapped my fork against my champagne glass, and everybody got quiet. Ms. Jane came and brought me the microphone.

"Thank you, everybody. I really appreciate the love y'all are showing us tonight. This is truly the happiest day of my life. Micah, I have a surprise for you. Ms. Jane, can you please hand me the envelope please?"

"Here you go." She handed it over to me. I gave it to Micah and watched as he opened it up. He pulled out the piece of paper.

"What's this?" He asked.

Talking into the microphone, I voiced, "I opened an after-care center for the kids in our old neighborhood. It's passed all its inspections and got all the permits, so it's set to open here soon. It's located right on Kessler next to the hair salon. It's named after both of our mothers, and Nookie, M-N-M After-Care Center."

Everyone started clapping, and Micah got up and gave me the tightest hug.

"That's wassup, babe. I really appreciate you, including my mom in that," Micah said into the mic.

"Anything for you. There's more, though." I giggled.

"Dang, I wonder what else it could be."

Micah dug his hand into the bottom of the manila envelope and pulled out the bracelet holder box. He looked confused at first until he opened it. His eyes got big as hell, "Are you forreal right now? Tell me you playing?" He pulled out the blue and white pregnancy test. "You're pregnant?"

Tears started forming in my eyes as I shook my head up and down. He picked me up and spun me around. He took the mic from me.

"I'mma be a daddy y'all! My baby's pregnant!" Everybody in the crowd started cheering.

"Congratulations, youngblood! My first grandchild!" OG yelled in excitement.

"Thank you for making me the happiest man alive." Micah hugged me again.

"No, thank you for making me a good woman again. Because of you, my heart has truly changed." I hugged him back, and we shared another sensual kiss.

This was my life from now on, and I was truly content with how everything turned out. I miss my best friend so much, and I wish she could share this happiness with me. I promise to look over her kids as if they were my own. I couldn't wait to raise them all together so that they cliqued up and never let people come against them. Love is a bitch, and when the heart and mind is at war, the heart damn near wins every time. The only thing is I'm certain that my heart and mind are on the same page, and that's with Micah Walker.

Epilogue

Casino

I made my way to the warehouse Bonnie used to own in Park 100. This would now be under my name and my business will be moving weight through there. I pulled up and saw Bonnie's Porsche already parked. I made my way inside and saw all the men and women that used to work under her patiently waiting. I also saw Mercedes standing alongside her.

"Wassup, y'all?"

"Hey, Casino, late as usual." Bonnie joked.

"My bad, them damn babies already attached to me, and they ain't even been home two months. How was the honeymoon?" I asked.

"It was great. Micah's got hella pictures, especially when we were swimming with them damn dolphins. But, let's get to it. We can chop it up later."

Bonnie made her way to the front of the room.

"Aight everybody, listen up. This is Casino. Most of y'all already know him. I am backing out of the game and will be turning everything over to him. I don't really need to explain anything to anyone about my decisions if you were at the wedding you kind of have an idea why I'm quitting. But, Casino will be a great leader to y'all, and I hope y'all can trust me enough to believe that."

She moved to the side, and I stepped up, "Does anyone have any issues with that?"

"I mean, Bonnie, how you think we're supposed to just accept somebody else coming in to take your place and it ain't one of us." A tall, dark-skinned dude came from the back of the crowd.

"I mean, it must be you that feels like you wanna take his place, Tank," Bonnie replied.

"Shit, I do," the nigga had the nerve to say.

"Come fight me for it then. Any nigga that can beat me can have this spot right here and now." I took off my hoodie and put it and my pistols that were in my waistband on the desk.

The nigga walked right up with his fists up, looking like he was ready to do some damage. He swung wildly, and I ducked that shit quick, and then I landed two blows to both sides of his ribs. He doubled over in pain. The nigga only had a punk ass t-shirt on, so I knew he felt those blows. That was the wrong move for him, though. I swept my leg under his, and he fell on his back, I pummeled blow after blow onto his face and head, he was literally getting all the built-up frustration, from losing Nookie to the babies being in the NICU, everything that I felt, he was feeling. Blood started to cover my hands and his face. I put him in a headlock that immediately put him to sleep. Everybody had looks of disgust in their face as if they were cringing the entire time — everybody but Bonnie and Mercedes. They knew how this shit worked.

I stood up and grabbed my hoodie, wiping off the blood on my hand.

"Anybody else wanna step up?" I looked around, and all you could see were people shaking their heads no. "That's what I thought. Play Russian roulette if you want to."

Nothing else was left to be said. I walked out and planned to become the biggest kingpin Nap ever seen.

The End